Time for Another?

Also by Tim Davidson:

Servants, Masters and Rogues formerly *The Bloomsbury Manuscript*
Music critic Hugo Belcher, in twenty-first century London, is a charming
rogue who, forever short of money, plans to marry a wealthy young heiress.
Meanwhile, Sandra Grisewood, a bright working-class girl, moves to London
where she hopes one day to realise her dream of becoming an opera singer.
Born in eighteenth-century Prague, music teacher Antonin Vasylicek, another
rogue and charmer, flees to England to evade his creditors and escape a
scandal. Their separate lives are, however, related in various ways, not least
the discovery of the score of an opera, based on Carlo Goldoni's comic play
'The Servant of Two Masters', which a renowned musicologist believes could
be a lost Mozart opera. There is an element of truth which provided the in-
spiration for this book, namely that Mozart was indeed writing or intending
to write a German opera based on Goldoni's play, for which a letter to his
father dated 5 February 1783 provides evidence, but no score has ever come
to light.

The Girl from Milan
The lives of a Bristol antique clock restorer and a beautiful researcher cross
paths at the grave of a long-dead British Army officer with a familiar name.
His curiosity piqued, Alec 'Tick-Tock' Fraser joins a quest with Silvia on
behalf of a wealthy Italian Count involving a roguish English baronet, a trip
to New York and a priceless cello, all to unravel a mystery – what happened
to the girl from Milan?

Time for a Party
A chance find in a village bookshop recalls an unspoken family history and
propels Geoff Mumford into a world of wealth, intrigue and promiscuity.
Visiting the South of France Geoff finds himself enmeshed in the story of
his glamorous forbear, only for the family history to be stolen in mysterious
circumstances...

Out of A Pale Blue Sky
William Wilkins is a history teacher at a minor public school in Gloucestershire and only son of a successful art dealer. Life in this quiet educational
backwater is pleasant and easy-going, ideally suited to William's unadven-
turous nature. His agreeable life and future prospects, however, are suddenly
overturned by a series of events coming without warning out of the blue.
Just as William's fortunes appear to be at their lowest ebb, some surprising
twists and turns occur setting his life on the road to recovery.

Time for Another?

Tim Davidson

This edition published in 2024 by Stephen Morris
www.stephen-morris.co.uk
© Tim Davidson
cover illustration ©Ceren Kara

ISBN 978-1-7396050-7-0

British Library Cataloguing-in-Publication Data
A catalogue record for this book is available from
the British Library

Contents

For my sons, Thomas and Nicholas

An Explanation

Time for Another? comprises a series of short stories all of which are related in the back bar of the Sloop Inn to the bar's most regular patrons (George, Tom, Desmond and the Colonel) by other customers. The regulars, too, have their own tales to tell spread throughout the book. The book is intended to be read as a novel, of which the stories are chapters designed to be read in the order in which they appear.

This is a new edition of the same title originally published in 2015, now fully revised and with additional stories.

Tim Davidson

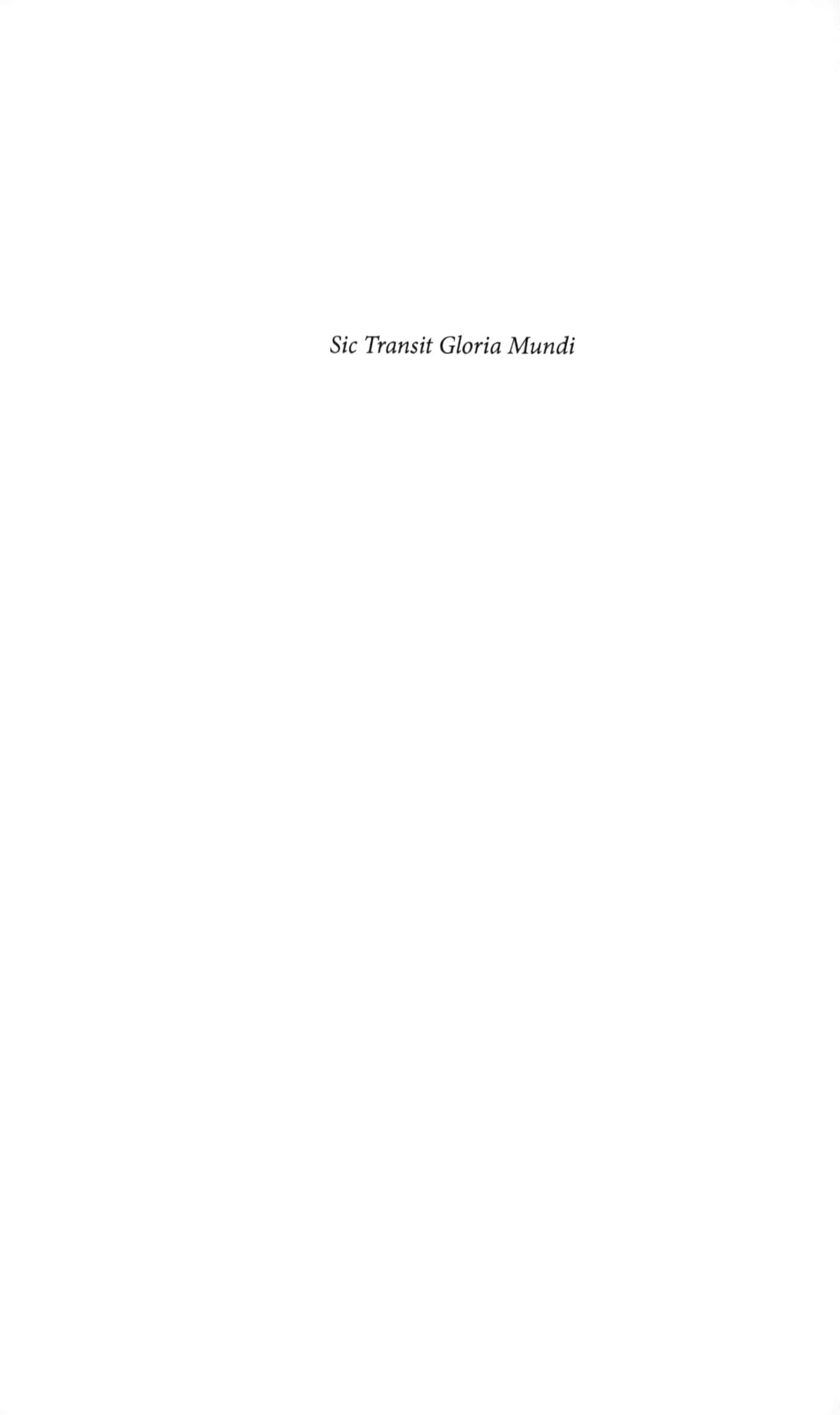

Sic Transit Gloria Mundi

At the Back Bar of the Sloop Inn

"Time for another, George? Tom asked.

"No thanks, Tom," I said, "Better not if you don't mind. We've got guests coming for dinner this evening and Molly will be very cross if I'm home late."

"Oh, come on – just a quick one … "

Well, of course, it's always 'just a quick one', isn't it? I mean to say, has anyone ever offered you a 'slow one', for goodness' sake?

"All right," I said. "I'll just have a quick one, then."

I was gathered with the other regulars, as usual of an evening, in the back bar of the Sloop Inn overlooking the harbour of our little town, Bufferton Regis, on the south Devon coast. Bufferton Regis is sometimes rather unkindly referred to as 'Old Bufferton Regis' on account of the average age of its residents. This is not entirely fair. For one thing the town attracts many tourists – or 'visitors' as the holiday industry prefers us to call them – of all classes and ages. Then, there are a growing number of second homeowners who come for weekends and of course the boating fraternity, too, who own yachts or motor cruisers moored at the marina. It is also worth recording that The Bufferton Sands Hotel on the sea front, until recently a rather ordinary seaside hotel, has now been converted into a more stylish venue boasting a much-vaunted, not to say expensive, new cocktail bar and seafood restaurant attracting guests of a younger and more cosmopolitan variety. That said, though, Bufferton, these days, is a primarily a place where middle class folk come to spend their retirement.

The Sloop has two bars – the Terrace and the Captain's – the latter generally referred to simply as the Back Bar. The Terrace Bar often becomes quite noisy and crowded and people looking for somewhere cosier and quieter usually make for the back bar – as indeed do the majority of the Sloop's regulars. And the most regular of the regulars are Tom, Gordon, Desmond and I.

We are all retired. Tom used to be an antiques dealer in the Cotswolds, Gordon was an army officer and is affectionately always referred to as the Colonel, Desmond, an Irishman, was the sales manager of a sportswear manufacturer in the Midlands, and I was formerly a partner in an old-established solicitors' practice in Surrey. Our select little group generally foregather at the bar every day in the early part of the evening. All of us are married, except for the Colonel, but our wives don't often visit the Sloop. I must confess that the atmosphere in the back bar is rather akin to that of an old-fashioned gentlemen's club, though of course ladies are most welcome, but, if we go out for a drink with our wives, it is normally to the chic new cocktail bar at the Bufferton Sands Hotel which is much more to their liking.

We regulars are perfectly capable of holding civilised and well-informed conversations about art, culture, current affairs and the like and sometimes indeed we do, but I regret to say that low humour never lurks far below the surface. It is rare for an evening to pass without an element of rude banter and a vulgar joke or two. After all, we are there to escape, to forget for a while the cares and irritations of daily life, to relax, to enjoy ourselves in easy-going company and to re-discover our inner schoolboy.

However, we try to make up for our many shortcomings by adopting a friendly approach to other patrons or visitors to our little bar and often, if we are lucky, we are rewarded with a story, sometimes a tale of woe, sometimes of joy. Some are tales of treachery or deception, some are quirky, some scandalous, some stories have happy endings and some not so happy. Whatever it is and however it ends, we all love a good story.

ONE

The Russian Bride

One of the pleasures of patronising the back bar at the Sloop was the uplifting sight behind the bar of Gloria, a splendid young woman in her late twenties, who until recently was our regular barmaid and whose cheerful service never failed to raise the spirits. If you were a writer and modelled the character of a fictional barmaid on Gloria, you would certainly be accused by critics of lazily resorting to stereotype: *a blonde, buxom barmaid.* Well, I mean to say. But that is what she was – an ash blonde, amply endowed, flirtatious barmaid. Altogether, she was as Desmond put it in his Irish way, *a wonder to behold.*

We were on our second round of drinks when a fellow in a stripy blazer came into the bar. We guessed – correctly – that he was the sort who would be staying at the Bufferton Sands Hotel. We wished him a polite *good evening* to which he responded with a smile and a nod, ordered his drink and moved to a vacant table nearby.

Continuing our conversation which focused, as it so often did, on matters of health and well-being, Tom confessed that he had been feeling rather low of late, but had summoned up the energy to take a bracing walk along the cliff path. By the time he returned, the clouds had lifted.

"Nothing like a good walk along the cliffs," he said, "to blow away the mental cobwebs."

The Colonel admitted that he too had got out of bed that morning feeling a bit grumpy. He had taken himself off for his usual morning coffee at the Copper Kettle Café in Fore Street where he had witnessed a clumsy waitress spill a double espresso over the trousers of the customer at the next table. The unfortunate victim happened to be a neighbour with whom the Colonel had recently had an acrimonious row over the siting of a new boundary fence. The incident at the café and the sight of the deep brown stain on the fellow's expensive white linen slacks had done much to improve the Colonel's temper, and he had given the waitress an especially generous tip.

I was about to extol the virtues of my own particular remedy for warding off a fit of the glooms, involving liberal doses of a decent white burgundy and Haydn's Trumpet Concerto, when the man in the stripy blazer butted in.

"I'm sorry to intrude upon your conversation," he said, "but I couldn't help overhearing what you were talking about and it reminded me of an old friend who adopted a rather more drastic strategy to counter the demons of depression. Perhaps you might like to hear about it?"

Well, of course we did! Tom bought the fellow a drink along with another round for the rest of us.

"Go ahead," I said. "We're all ears!"

"Well … " he began. It's extraordinary but so many stories we're told in the bar invariably begins with the word *well*, or sometimes, these days, *so* – which is very, indeed *so*, irritating.

WELL, THERE WERE THE FIVE OF US, thundering down the M4 in Malcolm's Range Rover on our annual pilgrimage to the England versus Wales rugby match, this year at the Millennium Stadium in Cardiff. We are a disparate bunch of chaps. Malcolm is a GP, Steve is a restaurateur, Guy is in marketing, Ted runs a local garden centre and I – Douglas by the way – practise as an independent financial advisor. However we have in common that, in our youth, we all played for the same local rugby club, which we still support, and secondly that we are all regulars – much too regular in fact – at the Gravediggers' Arms, our local pub.

To pass the time on the journey, we took it in turn to tell jokes and stories. These fell broadly into three categories – jokes about the Welsh, jokes about sex, and scurrilous stories about people we know, which may or may not be entirely true.

My story, when it came to my turn, fell into the latter category, but for once I was sure that the facts were absolutely correct and required no embellishment at all on my part.

"Do you remember my old friend and former golfing partner, Maurice Lombard?" I asked.

Of course they remembered him. Once met, it would frankly be difficult to forget him. Maurice was a flamboyant sort of chap – natty dresser, vintage Jag, always with some racy lady on his arm, different one each time. They hadn't seen him, though, for some long while, any more than I had until recently, and I was able to divulge that, about a year or so before, Maurice, formerly the most committed of bachelors, got himself married to a young woman. Maurice was 61 years old when he met her and the young lady was just 24.

Gasps of astonishment echoed round the assembled company. I could tell that they all wanted to hear more of the story.

I'm afraid that it's a rather sad tale. It didn't end well for Maurice, and, as always, there are lessons to be learnt, though regrettably, in my experience, they rarely are.

He had always been a jovial, larger than life character. If you were feeling a bit low all you needed was a brief infusion of Maurice to set you right again, like a welcome glass of champagne. Come to think of it, Maurice and champagne often came together for not only was he a bubbly sort of fellow but also a prolific party giver and a most generous host.

Maurice was the proprietor of a prosperous company supplying office equipment and a pillar of the local community. One day, however, he received a substantial offer for the business which was much too tempting to refuse. The sale proceeded and Maurice went to live at a place called Biggleton-on-Sea on the Sussex coast to spend more time with his yacht. After that, we all lost touch with him, and it was only by chance that I bumped into him in a restaurant in London. He was on his own and invited me to join him, and over a long and boozy lunch, he related his dreadful tale of woe in all its lurid detail, utterly baring his soul and omitting nothing however embarrassing.

It was not long after Maurice's retirement to the seaside, once the euphoria of the sale of his business had subsided, that he began to find life a little tedious. He missed the cut and thrust of business dealings. The very lack of any cause of stress paradoxically became itself a cause of stress. It's funny how life's changes creep up on you without you really noticing. Thus, it was that, one morning, he looked at himself in his bedroom mirror and instead of the debonair man about town with a slightly raffish air that he imagined himself to be, and indeed had been, the reflection that stared back at him was of a balding elderly man in an ill-fitting suit with a paunch. The fact that it was a burgundy bulge rather than a beer belly was of little consolation. A paunch is a paunch. Furthermore, he realised, he was missing the company of his old chums and business colleagues. The sad simple facts were that he had become a bored, lonely, fat, old-looking man.

Introspection did not come easily to him. Life was for living not for thinking about, but after an hour or two of solemn reflection he had reached a devastating conclusion – if he was to avoid descending into a sad and lonely dotage, he must take a wife! There was still time, he told himself, if he smartened himself up. Given a pretty young woman, he was sure he could rise, as it were, to the occasion. It would be the saving of him, and he would have company when he most needed it.

Over lunch at the Yacht Club that day, he negligently let slip his intentions. His fellow members thought he was mad even to contemplate marriage. It would be like being back at boarding school, constantly scolded by Matron over the smallest of things. He'd be nagged into an early grave. The club treasurer took the view that, as a man of the world, he must know what was best for him, but urged caution. Maurice was obviously a wealthy individual and the world was full of gold-diggers. All were of the view that, if he was determined on this course, he must find a lady of mature years. The names of suitable local widows were bandied about with their respective credentials. The overall favourite was Grace, the widow of the former town clerk. Admittedly she had run to fat a little of late, but she still played a mean hand of bridge, her flower arrangements were legendary, and her rhubarb crumble was beyond reproach.

But Maurice would have none of this. He had set his heart, not to mention other parts of his anatomy, on a young woman and a young woman it would be. So there!

The trouble was the old sexual magnetism seemed to have deserted him. An attempt to engage a pair of attractive girls in the Hare & Tortoise in conversation was not so much rebuffed as ignored. A tall brunette waiting in the rain at the bus stop outside Sainsbury's, to whom he chivalrously offered a lift, accused him of sexual harassment. Somehow, he didn't quite like the idea of a dating agency, but what else could he do?

Quite fortuitously, one afternoon while waiting his turn at the hairdressers, Maurice chanced upon a newspaper article entitled *Young Russian brides on the Internet*. It struck him immediately – here was the solution! Modern English girls now were so, well – *modern*. A nice Russian girl, grateful for the chance of a new life in the West, would surely be more appreciative of his old-fashioned charm and more likely to make a respectful and obedient wife.

Unfamiliar with the mysteries of the internet, Maurice hastened next day to Winchester where his nephew William lived. William would have the means to help him pursue his romantic cyber-quest and, sure enough, three weeks later Maurice was on board a British Airways flight destined for St. Petersburg, where it had been arranged that he should meet Olga.

Olga greeted him at the airport. Much to his surprise, she spoke excellent English and was plainly a well-educated young lady. But what really mattered was that she was unquestionably the most ravishingly beautiful girl he had ever seen. His mind was made up, and in the gardens of the Peterhof Palace, on bended knee, he proposed marriage and was instantly accepted.

On his next visit to Russia, the couple were duly joined in wedlock at a brief civil ceremony and flew immediately to Paris for their honeymoon. The discreet little establishment on the Left Bank which Maurice had chosen for their stay did not, however, much appeal to Olga and a move was arranged to a very elegant and expensive hotel close to the Place Vendôme, near the best shops. The cost of the whole affair was eye-watering but Maurice, besotted with his new bride, hardly blinked.

At last, the couple arrived in England and settled down to their new life. Each morning, they visited a smart local health and fitness club as Maurice needed to keep in trim for the performance of his new marital duties. He soon gave up on the exercise machines, but enjoyed the swimming pool and especially the Jacuzzi where Olga always joined him after her aerobic session. He simply couldn't resist fondling her gorgeous body in the warm, bubbly water, quite oblivious to onlookers. The onlookers were not, of course, oblivious to Olga, in particular a young man called

Damian. Olga had noticed him too. He resembled one of those macho types who model expensive skiwear and sport a permanent tan. Often, he sat close to her in the Jacuzzi so their thighs touched even as Maurice pawed and petted her. Soon they were lovers. Everyone in the town knew, except poor Maurice – for Maurice was quite blind with infatuation.

One day, he returned from lunch at the Yacht Club earlier than usual and found them making love on the patio. His eyes temporarily opened, he raged and shouted at them, but Olga stood her ground. He was imagining things, she said. As always, he had had too much to drink and his mind was confused. Soon he was tearfully apologising for doubting her and grovelling for forgiveness.

Maurice indulged Olga's every wish. She demanded financial independence and he paid her a substantial monthly allowance. His comfortable house was transformed into an exotic version of a Russian dacha, all to make her feel more at home. She found Biggleton-on-Sea a little dull, so he bought her a flat in London, to which she could escape whenever she wished, and where, of course, unbeknown to him, she continued her passionate affair with Damian.

Very occasionally, recapturing a vestige of his old spirit, he dared to question some new whim or fancy, but Olga simply stared at him with her beautiful, cold, blue eyes. An icy silence descended like the eerie stillness of a Russian winter until, with a flick of her long dark hair and the most spectral of smiles, she turned on her heel and walked slowly towards the bedroom. Maurice followed a few steps behind, his face resuming an expression of quasi-religious devotion.

What heroin is to an addict, Olga was to Maurice. It was tragic for such a good man to fall under the spell of such a woman, blind to her infidelity until too late, a cuckold and a slave.

⁎

A thoughtful silence descended following the end of my story, broken first by Ted who quoted that sage old proverb: *there's no such fool as an old fool,* with which Guy, Malcolm and I hastened to agree.

Steve, however, remained silent, looking a trifle uncomfortable and somewhat red in the face.

I asked him what he thought about the matter.
He was reluctant at first to say anything at all, but finally, in an apologetic tone of voice, he said: "I meant to tell you chaps before but Nanette and I are engaged to be married."

Nanette was a pretty young French waitress employed at Steve's restaurant. Hers were the long, shapely legs that had *launched a thousand fantasies* – as one wag had put it.

Nanette would be about the same age as Olga was when she married Maurice, and Steve is quite old enough to be her father.

None of the rest of us knew quite what to say.

TWO

The Cyclops Machine

A bitter blow for all of us regulars at the Sloop Inn: Gloria, our lovely barmaid, announced that she would be leaving to take up a new job at a hotel in Exeter for more money.

"Sic transit Gloria mundi," as Tom put it, with a deep sigh.

A new girl would be coming to take over during the summer months, and the landlord would be looking for a permanent replacement from October onwards.

So distracted were we by the news of Gloria's departure that we didn't even notice a fellow enter the bar until he spoke to order a drink. We wished him a cheery *good evening* which he acknowledged with a barely perceptible nod before moving off with his drink to a table by the window where he proceeded to fiddle with some curious gizmo attached to his wrist. After a bit, he took out from his rucksack one of those tablet things with which he began to play. He seemed entirely engrossed with these devices and completely oblivious to his surroundings or the view from the window. We shrugged and resumed our conversation.

We were talking about the summer drinks party at the Golf and Croquet Club the previous evening which had been a great success, and Desmond asked if the rest of us would be going to the fireworks display at the harbour which was scheduled to take place on the following Saturday.

Tom said that he heard that the Council were planning to put up more of *those wretched CCTV cameras* along the harbour walkway.

The subject of CCTV cameras always seems to divide opinion.

Desmond and the Colonel thought they were a necessary evil, but Tom and I disagreed. This inevitably led on to a general discussion of the issues of snooping and intrusion by officialdom and its agencies.

While we're on the subject of snooping, Tom said he'd heard a rumour from a friend who worked for a security firm about some new device called a Cyclops Machine which will apparently be much more sophisticated and intrusive than CCTV, but it was all a big secret at the moment and details were sketchy.

At the mention of the Cyclops Machine, the chap with the funny wrist contraption suddenly came to life. The bar is quite small, and unless it is full of people, one can hear what anyone is saying if you care to listen.

"I could tell you something about the Cyclops Machine," he said. "I've some personal experience of it."

Putting away his tablet and picking up his drink, he came to join us at the bar, introducing himself as David. He had, he told us, been attending a business conference in Exeter. It had ended quite late and, rather than drive all the way back to Berkshire where he lived, he had decided to stay locally. He could have booked into the conference hotel, but had chosen to travel down to Bufferton for old times' sake because he'd spent many happy holidays here as a child with his parents ... Perhaps, I thought, he's not such a bad chap after all.

"I'm afraid," he said, "I'm a complete sucker for all these wonderful digital devices."

"Yes, we guessed!" Tom said.

"But these things have their drawbacks and dangers," the fellow went on, "as even I've come to realise. Perhaps you'd like to hear the story of how I came to discover the Cyclops Machine?"

"We certainly would!" Tom said, and we all murmured our agreement.

Well, let me start with the day I visited my mother. It was not so long ago and I remember the conversation very clearly. It was so typical of my mother, and this is how it went, more or less word for word:

"David, darling, what on earth is that thing?" She asked.

"What thing, Mother?" I said.

"That peculiar bracelet thing on your wrist. It's not some sort of religious symbol, is it? You haven't joined one of those weird cults or some secret society, have you?"

"Don't be silly, Mother. It's my new Pixie."

"Well, it doesn't look like a pixie, dear. Pixies are naughty little fairies who live at the bottom of gardens, mainly in Cornwall, I believe." She said.

I told her that it had got nothing to do with that sort of pixie. I explained that it was a smart watch and its technical name was a Personal Information and Communications Straplet – but that everyone called them Pixies.

They are widely regarded, I believe, to be one of the best smart watches currently available on the market, combining the functions of a mobile phone, personal organizer, digital radio, camera, instant internet access, messaging and email, while providing a wide variety of other features and facilities. It can also give an instant read-out of your blood pressure, pulse rate and cholesterol level, and naturally tells you the time in whatever time zone you wish. As it is obviously too small to incorporate a keypad, it is entirely voice-activated once you have selected the appropriate mode by pressing one of the little buttons on the outer rim.

I tried to explain all this to Mother but she gave me one of her funny looks. I could tell that she was not in the slightest bit interested.

"Whatever will they think of next? A mind-reading machine, I shouldn't wonder!" she said, before offering me another gingerbread man. She always makes gingerbread men especially for me whenever I go to see her.

Much Tangle, where my mother lives in a wisteria-clad house called The Spinney, is certainly an attractive Berkshire village. Its winding main street leads to a row of attractive cottages and some rather grander Georgian houses clustered around a large village green. The imposing thirteenth-century church of St. Ninian is set discreetly back at one end of the green while the local pub, the Goose and Gander, lies at the opposite end. It might not be quite striking enough to feature on the lids of biscuit tins sold in National Trust shops, but it is certainly very pretty and full of old-world charm.

I duly polished off my gingerbread man and finally drove away along the narrow road leading out of the village. I couldn't help thinking of the great contrast there was between Much Tangle and the Astra 21 Digital Village, where my wife Myra and I had recently purchased an ultra-modern 'executive' home, number 16A Laser Drive. Built on the outskirts of Mowlesbury adjacent to the new link road with excellent connections to the motorway and Mowlesbury Parkway Station, Astra 21 is a new concept in residential development. It might be only half an hour's drive from Much Tangle, but I mused as I motored along, it is absolutely a world apart in every other way. Indeed, one might say that it occupies a completely different culture zone.

In fact, the journey took a little longer than normal. I couldn't resist using the car's satnav although I knew the way of course perfectly well. It was just such a brilliant bit of kit and I was absolutely thrilled with it. The machine had taken me by a quite different route from my usual one and I had unfortunately ended up in a country lane, even narrower than the road to Much Tangle, where I'd become stuck behind a large articulated lorry which had been unable to negotiate a tight corner. This sort of thing happens too often – these little country roads really ought to be widened. Very frustrating! As it was, a kind local farmer allowed me to drive through his farmyard to avoid the lorry and then directed me down a farm track. This came out onto another lane, and the satnav, now understandably confused, had directed me to turn right. The farmer had told me to turn left when I reached the lane and I decided that I'd better do as he advised. Feeling guilty, I, of course, apologised to her – my satnav that is – for disobeying her well-meaning instructions.

At last, I reached the Astra 21 village and approached Network Avenue, the principal estate road. The security barrier automatically lifted to let me pass as the electronic sensor recognised my car. Likewise, the garage door opened up for me as I turned into Laser Drive. I was, though, mildly surprised to notice that the Automow, which was programmed automatically to mow the lawn whenever the grass reaches a certain length, was in operation again when I arrived. It had only cut the grass just the day before and, though no expert in horticultural matters, I somehow doubted that grass could grow quite that quickly. Puzzling. Very puzzling.

On entering the house by way of the connecting door at the rear of the garage, the DVA, which stands for Digital Voice Announcer by the way, blared forth:

Myra has arrived. Myra has arrived. Welcome home, Myra!

This was most disappointing. Why, I sighed inwardly, could the damn DVA not identify me correctly? It was linked up properly to the camera monitors and I was quite sure that I'd programmed the system correctly in accordance with the instruction manual.

Then, my wife appeared, with a contemptuous look on her face.

"Hello, Myra!" she said pointedly,

Myra likes to tease me. She suggested that, as we'd apparently swapped names, we should swap clothes too. She said she was rather tired of the pink dress that she was wearing – it made her look frumpy – but perhaps it might suit me?

Doing my best to ignore the heavy sarcasm, I told her that one had to expect a few teething problems with sophisticated technology like this. It was the price of progress.

Myra was absolutely scathing. She complained that she couldn't even sit out in the garden that afternoon for fear, as she put it, of "that vicious thing suddenly bounding out of its lair to demolish the few remaining blades of grass on our front lawn." What if she had been asleep in a deck chair, she said, and it had barged into her? It might have chopped her into little pieces! "Was this", she ranted, "the price of progress?"

A trifle ruffled, I offered to go down to the control room immediately and alter the computerised settings.

"Don't you dare," she said, reminding me that the last time I had tried to make some adjustment I had, by mistake, triggered a security alert – and the Digital Voice Announcer in the hall declared that the area was in imminent danger of a terrorist attack with biological weapons. Great steel shutters came down sealing off all the windows and doors and we were sprayed with some pungent disinfectant for twenty minutes. I have to admit that the carpets and furniture still emit a slight smell.

Instead, Myra suggested that we should go out onto the patio and chill out together with a nice Campari Soda. She said it would take away the taste of my mother's *horrid little gingerbread biscuits* – as she rather rudely described them.

As we sipped our Campari Sodas, she mentioned that my friend Rory had phoned. He wanted us all to meet up on Saturday at the usual café in Mowlesbury. Rory works for an IT company, heading up their research and development department. All very state-of-the-art and cutting edge. He was undoubtedly a high-flyer in the industry and I always enjoyed our little chats. Myra added that Rory apparently had something interesting to show me. "Probably," she said, "yet another bloody electronic contraption."

***

Saturday came at last. We met up with Rory and his wife, Liz, at the River Terrace Wine Bar and Café in the old centre of Mowlesbury, our usual rendezvous. Myra and Liz didn't stay long but went off shopping together, leaving Rory and I at a table on the attractive open-air terrace overlooking the river. Why Myra wouldn't use the internet for her shopping needs I could never really understand – so much more convenient and in keeping with progressive trends, allowing time for ... well ... er ... sitting in the garden, texting friends, doing the household accounts on the tablet or whatever, while waiting for the supermarket delivery van to arrive, but she would have none of it. She once remarked that if she had to live in a house which she described as *a cross between a high security prison, a district hospital and the interior of a nuclear submarine*, then, at least, she must at least be allowed to go to the shops occasionally and meet, as she put it, *some normal human beings*.

I didn't argue, but secretly felt quite hurt by Myra's attitude. Did she not think, then, that I was a normal human being?! Really!

Well, to be fair, I reflected, the shopping expedition did at least give Rory and I the opportunity to spend an hour or so by ourselves.

The conversation on these occasions tended, unsurprisingly, to focus upon the latest items of digital wizardry available on the market. It was Rory, in fact, who had persuaded me to buy a Pixie at what he claimed to be the bargain price of £899.99 – "inclusive of VAT." I remember the conversation on that Saturday with particular clarity, and the memory of the events on that fateful day and the days that followed will remain forever stored on the hard-drive of my mind.

Having placed our order for coffee and a brace of fudge brownies, Rory produced a small black plastic box and put it on the table.

This was the thing that he had wanted to show me, he said.

Bemused but excited, I asked what it was.

In answer, he opened the box and took from it what looked to all intents and purposes like an American baseball cap. I was still mystified.

Rory smiled and turned the cap over to reveal the inside of it, which was lined with some sort of lightly padded material. A little unusual for a baseball cap, I thought, but so what?

Rory winked at me and pulled off the interior lining, which I could see now had only been attached to the inside edge of the cap by a few strips of Velcro. Inside the cap, previously concealed by the lining, was a network of small electrodes connected by thin wires to each other and to a flat unit about the same size and shape as a mini pocket calculator. Next, Rory turned the cap the other way up so I could take a close look at the outside of it. It seemed quite like a normal cap, except that in the middle above the peak where one might have expected to see a team badge or some other logo there was instead a round, semi-transparent object like a large glass eye.

I was still completely puzzled, however.

"Here, try it on," Rory urged, passing it to me but without putting back the lining.

Gingerly, I did as I was asked.

Next, he instructed me to look at anybody on this terrace,

suggesting a man in the far corner sitting on his own, a podgy chap with a red face. He told me to try to concentrate on looking at him without thinking of anything else and keep my head as still as I could.

I did as Rory told me. A very slight feeling of dizziness overcame me for a moment or two, and then the most extraordinary thing happened. I started to think about football. I never in ordinary circumstances think about football. I'm not, frankly, the sporty type and honestly the game doesn't interest me. But here I was in a football stadium with huge stands on each side and at either end, each crammed to capacity with fans. I was running forward, and the ball was passed to me from the wing. It was not a good pass but expertly I managed to control the ball and dribbled it, if that is the word, deftly first past one and then another of the defending team. They didn't stand a chance, poor devils, such was the elusive brilliance of my footwork. I took a shot at goal. The goalkeeper was hopelessly wrong-footed and the ball sailed into the back of the net. The crowd went wild. The other players on my team rushed forward to mob and hug me in the way that footballers do and I was lifted up on someone's shoulders. The roar from the fans was deafening – I was a hero!

Just at this moment, Janet, our charming waitress, came over to take my order. All sight and sound of football suddenly faded from my thoughts ...

It was simply unbelievable! Janet now seemed to be wearing a very skimpy bikini and I was entertaining thoughts about her of a most licentious nature. Oh dear, the shame of it.

But of course, Janet, as I dimly realised in the far reaches of my consciousness, wasn't really taking my order, let alone wearing a bikini. It was all the pure fantasy of this podgy chap. In reality, she was just standing there by his table patiently waiting for his order, with her little notebook in hand and pencil poised.

Nevertheless, I flushed with embarrassment.

I, or rather my podgy alter ego, chose to order *a pot of tea and one of them chocolate sponge things* and Janet went off in the direction of the kitchen. Almost immediately I was back again in the football stadium, this time about to take a free kick. The crowd was silent. It was a moment of high drama. I ran up and kicked the ball. Its curving trajectory took it safely past the wall of defenders. The keeper took a despairing leap at it to no avail – it was another magnificent goal!

It was all too much. Enough! Some instinct made me tear the cap from my head. The football stadium was instantly erased from my mind and, after another short spell of dizziness, I returned to something like normal.

Quite overcome with astonishment, I could barely speak.

"Amazing device, isn't it?" Rory said, smiling. He explained that his company had developed the original prototype and holds the patent on it. Officially it was called an Electronic Cerebral Impulse Reflector but it had become known in the business as the Cyclops Machine after the one-eyed giant of ancient Greek myth. "We all know," he proclaimed, "about people who hack into computers, but with this new device one can now hack into someone's brain." That's *precisely*, he said, what I had been doing just then with our fat friend in the far corner. I was thinking his thoughts.

I simply couldn't believe it, and asked how on earth it worked.

Rory explained that the technology was quite sophisticated but he put it in as simple terms as he could: Apparently, when we think our brains emit a series of tiny electrical impulses. The Cyclops Machine sends out a highly directional electronic beam, a sort of radar beam. If the Cyclops operator is within 30 metres of a target individual and the beam is accurately focused, it will pick up these little impulses, convert them into digital signals and bounce them back, via the glass eye, to the receptor inside the cap. The signals are then automatically decoded and transmitted via the electrodes into the operator's own brain where they manifest themselves as the original thoughts or mental visions running through the target's mind.

"Good God!" Was all I could say.

Rory informed me that the Cyclops has been on secret trial in the United States now for about a year. At present, its use would be restricted to the CIA and the FBI for counter-terrorism operations, but the security services of other governments and police forces worldwide would naturally be interested ... and probably big business too. It's all a bit hush-hush at the moment but, if it all goes ahead, Rory's company frankly stands to make millions out of this invention.

I suggested that there might be problems with human rights legislation and all that sort of thing. Rory was convinced, however, that the authorities would find a way round all that. They'd claim some sort of exemption, the interests of national security or whatever. Eventually, little by little, the exemption would be extended to anything which is deemed to be in the public interest, deemed, that is, by the government. Policeman and politicians, he was sure, were certainly not going to miss out on such a fantastic opportunity of spying on everyone and finding out what we all really think. This would surely be the ultimate surveillance tool.

I expressed concern that we were using this thing in a café. Ought it not to be kept under lock and key?

Rory replied that I was quite right strictly speaking, but he had a spare machine knocking about in his office and frankly he just couldn't resist the temptation to play with it. Of course, he'd only shown it off to a few old friends like me on whose discretion he could rely. That was his excuse any way. Then he invited me to have another go.

I was very reluctant at first, but, in the end, he persuaded me. A little nervously I put the thing on again. This time I didn't feel dizzy at all and found that I could actually maintain a few parallel thoughts of my own alongside the incoming thoughts, as it were, though sometimes the two trains of thought became confused or merged with one another.

First, I focused on a young man of student age. He was contemplating whether to spend his gap year working on a fish farm in Alaska, or at an elephant sanctuary in Tamil Nadu. I didn't particularly envy him these choices and moved on to a smartly dressed middle-aged gentleman sitting at a table with two women, who were nattering away with each other, while the gentleman was doing the crossword.

Five Down: suitable side dish for an astronaut, perhaps – two words, first word six letters, second word five letters.

Suddenly, he looked up in the direction of the main road running passed the café. A classic vintage sports car was driving by and had obviously caught his attention. The crossword puzzle disappeared and I, or rather the be-whiskered gentleman, imagined himself at the wheel of this splendid vehicle. I/he was driving along a scenic road with mountains to one side and a dazzling blue sea on the other. It looked to me like the famous drive along Amalfi coast in Italy.

Again, in a flash as quickly as it had come, the image of the car and the beautiful scenery evaporated.

Got it! Rocket salad! Now, for four across, the third letter must, therefore, be k ...

Bored with crosswords, I turned to direct the Cyclops at an elderly lady at the opposite end of the terrace. It was my mother! What in God's name, I thought, was she doing here? Then I remembered. As one of the few residents of Much Tangle who still drove a car, she had offered to take her neighbour, Dora Watson, to the chiropodist. The chiropodist's premises were quite close by and no doubt she was waiting for Dora to finish her treatment. Plainly she hadn't noticed me. As usual she was in her own little dream world.

Soon mother's thoughts presented themselves in my mind. The chairman of the parish council and his wife were coming to tea. *What should she give them*, she was wondering? *Gingerbread men, of course! Ah, but that might not be enough and what if they didn't like them? Better buy a lemon sponge just in case.*

In an instant, all thoughts of tea were forgotten. Instead, the old soul was in the company of a tall distinguished-looking Asian gentleman. They were seated facing each other on a magic carpet flying high over a fairy-tale city of jewel-like domes and pink minarets. Mother was dressed in a strangely eccentric garment – half sari, half English summer frock – a sort of Home Counties meets the Punjab creation. I recognised the Asian gentleman immediately – it was Mr. Choudhury, proprietor of the corner shop in Much Tangle where, presumably, she intended to buy the lemon sponge. Well, really!

Rory's voice broke into these strange dreams. It felt to me as if he was speaking on the telephone at long distance on a bad line, even though he was sitting right next to me. He proposed that we had a drink before the girls got back, a proper one this time – a glass of wine.

I removed the Cyclops, put it back on the table, and hastened to accept Rory's suggestion

Janet was summoned to fetch a couple of glasses of the South African *Chenin Blanc*.

When the drinks arrived, Rory asked if I'd like to borrow the Cyclops for a few days. He could come and pick it up from me sometime the following week. His voice sounded quite normal again. He could see, he claimed, that I was really beginning to enjoy it and, I have to admit, that despite my earlier reservations indeed I was.

He'd been playing with it all week, he said, and his wife was getting a bit pissed off with him. He would trust me to be very careful with it and not to show it to anyone else.

And, so I finally agreed to borrow the thing.

****

A little while later, Liz and Myra returned from shopping at just about the same time as Dora Watson arrived after her session at the chiropodist to meet my mother. On their way out, mother finally noticed me and waved.

Waving back to her I asked her to give my regards to Mr. Choudhury, at which Myra gave me a quizzical look, but I said nothing.

Then, she noticed the box containing the Cyclops machine and asked what it was.

Rory told her that it was only one of his new toys, which he'd allowed me borrow for a few days, while he smiled at me conspiratorially.

Myra gave me another of her funny looks.

****

Monday came. I've always hated Mondays. The working week seems a bit like a long sea crossing in a very slow boat with the weekend but a distant shore, only just visible on the horizon. That morning, though, was a little different. I had taken the Cyclops to work with me.

From my room, there is a good view, if the door is left open, of the outer office, as it is called. The outer office accommodated the office manager, the accounts executive and the secretarial work stations. It was easy for me to spy on anyone I wished, and spy I duly did.

First, I trained the Cyclops on Jack Eccles, the office manager and general factotum, hoping for something of interest, but Jack was only contemplating what next to plant on his allotment. Would there be room for cabbages as well as runner beans? Nothing of great interest.

Next it was the turn of the secretaries. Doreen was, it transpired, deeply in love with Clive, the new management trainee, and nurtured hopes of unmentionable things happening to her behind the cricket pavilion at next Friday's annual match against the firm's accountants. Lucy was re-living her previous night's clubbing. She was very concerned that an unmentionable thing might already have happened to her in the club car park, but she had had so much to drink by that stage that she couldn't really remember exactly what or with whom. Jenny was contemplating handing in her notice so that she could go to work for the local branch of a building society where the money was better. The only thing restraining her from this course of action was that she was also deeply in love with Clive and the thought that if she left now, she'd be *making it, like, easier for that cow Doreen to get 'er claws into 'im*. The other two girls both harboured similar feelings and hopes of unmentionable things happening to them at Clive's doing as both Doreen and Jenny. Clive, it seemed, was going to be a very busy young man. I wondered if he knew.

This left only Greta, the accounts executive. Greta was an intelligent, well-spoken girl and, I think, most attractive too. In the short time she had been with the firm I had grown, I have to confess, rather fond of her. Indeed, from the engaging way she often smiled at me, I had dared to hope that my feelings were, in some small measure, reciprocated. Out of my regard and affection for her, I hesitated at first to intrude upon her privacy, but in the end, of course, curiosity got the better of me. Donning the Cyclops once more, I focused it on her. Just as I did so, she happened to look in my direction.

What's that old fart staring at me for? She was thinking as she flashed me one of her sweetest of smiles, *and why's he wearing that funny hat?*

***

I left the office earlier than usual that day and was sitting at home in my favourite armchair waiting for the early evening news on the television.

Still somewhat saddened by the revelation that Greta considered me of no greater account than an expulsion of stale bodily air from the anal passage, I was wondering what I had done to deserve her low opinion of me. Myra had brought me a cup of tea which I was sipping while trying to find some way to shake off my dismal mood. From the symbol appearing in the corner of the mini-screen of my Pixie, it seemed that there were some new messages for me. Well here, at least, was something to distract me, but though I assiduously followed the procedure for accessing messages set out in the instruction booklet, or at least thought I had, the thing kept flipping onto the internet and all that emerged was the weather forecast for a place called Daytona Beach in Florida. Several times I tried but always with the same result, except on the last occasion when an advertisement appeared for a car auction in Swansea. It was all most irritating.

With a sigh of resignation, I idly chanced to look out of the French window and saw Myra hanging out the washing, draping it over the new garden furniture which we had recently purchased at B&Q. Much to my chagrin, the Automow suddenly hove into view, cutting away again. Myra broke off from what she was doing just long enough to throw a chair at it, before resuming her task. Why did she do it? Hanging out the washing, I wondered, when we had an Automaid robot which could be programmed to do the whole job, even the pressing and ironing. Most peculiar!

Sighing once more, my attention turned back to the Cyclops Machine. which was lying next to the telephone on the top of a small bookcase near the window. I thought of putting it on again to focus on Myra to learn exactly what was going through her mind, but I didn't do so. Somehow it just seemed unfair, the wrong thing to do. In fact, I had now come to regret ever using the bloody thing.

I found myself wondering what George Orwell would have made of it if the Cyclops Machine had been invented when he wrote *Nineteen Eighty-Four* and coined the idea of a 'thoughtcrime'. Is that where all this could lead?

Perhaps, Myra was right all along, I mused. The price of progress may sometimes be too high. Would it not be better, I asked myself, if the atomic bomb had never been invented, let alone the Cyclops machine?

Just then, the telephone rang. It was Rory. He said he'd been trying to get hold of me. He'd texted me twice, but got no reply, so he'd had no alternative but to use this "obsolete form of communication" as he put it. I assumed that he wanted to fix a time to come and pick up the Cyclops Machine, but no, he didn't.

He told me that his boss at work had accused him of a breach of company rules by keeping one of the Cyclops Machines in his office in full view and taking it home with him, when it should have been returned to the research lab and locked away. This was quite true of course, but Rory had vigorously denied it, claiming that it was not the Cyclops Machine but a fancy baseball cap intended as a birthday present for his son.

"Best you keep it for the time being, David, until I can find a way of smuggling it back to the research lab without anyone noticing. Just hide it away somewhere safe."

"I'll do better than that," I replied emphatically. "I'll destroy the bloody thing!"

Before Rory could say anything more, I replaced the receiver, and picking up the Cyclops machine, I dropped it on the floor just below me. Then I proceeded to stamp on it as hard as I could three or four times.

At the last stamp, with a most satisfying crunch, the horrid, sinister glass eye shattered into thousand glittering fragments.

One hopes that the use of this dreadful device will never be legally permitted, but, if it ever should be, I would strongly advise you all to beware of policeman wearing baseball caps.

THREE

The Diary

It was very wrong of us, I know, to read someone else's diary without their consent, but there it is – we did.

But first things first – the evening we found the diary was the first evening on which the new barmaid was on duty in our bar. We stood there, not exactly drooling, but certainly wide-eyed and open-mouthed. Emily was her name, and she was – and no other words will do – a truly beautiful young woman with the loveliest pair of big blue eyes and the most angelic face you can imagine. She was intelligent, charming and anxious to please and the warmth of her smile would melt the Arctic ice cap faster than any amount of global warming.

Desmond, his Irish brogue growing thicker by the minute, babbled away about how the Lord had bestowed upon us this great bounty and all because he had put a tenner in the collection plate at church on Sunday instead of a fiver by mistake. I bought a round and we were toasting our good fortune when Tom noticed that something had been left behind on the table by the door at which two people, a man and a woman, had been sitting. He went to fetch it.

"Look," he said, "it's a diary and must belong to the bloke, the one who was just sitting there, see his name, Martin, is engraved here on the cover. Let's just see if there's some address or telephone number inside." Tom had a good flip through. "No, there doesn't seem to be, but, hey, hey, this isn't just any sort of diary, you know, with dinner engagements and dental appointments, this is a proper job – a day-by-day account of the chap's life by the look of it. Come on, let's have a little look, shall we?"

"We shouldn't really," I said, but without much conviction, and was promptly and unanimously overruled. Tom has a mellifluous if slightly plummy tone of voice, like an old-fashioned BBC Third Programme presenter. He settled himself back on his bar stool and opened the diary at random. "Well, here goes," he said, and began to read out loud:

Thursday April 17th

Dropped a valuable first edition of The Pickwick Papers this morning and damaged the cover. 'Bugger, Bugger, Bugger!' I said to myself out loud, not realising that there was a customer in the shop, a rather posh lady, who asked for a copy of Stories from the Arabian Nights illustrated by Edmund Dulac, which she wanted to give as a present to her niece on her birthday.

I normally keep several copies of the Dulac version of the Arabian Nights in various editions, but of course I didn't have one in stock today – a good sale gone begging! Bugger, Bugger, Bugger!

Yet another semi-row with Marcia when I got home for supper! I was not to forget, she said, about collecting Caroline from her piano lesson tomorrow evening. I protested that I was supposed to be going to a drinks party. 'Well,' she insisted in her usual peremptory manner, 'you'll just have to say you're sorry you can't go, won't you? I've reminded you about Caroline's lesson at least three times and I'm going to the theatre with Sylvie tomorrow, so I can't collect her myself.' And that was that.

It has been a bad week so far and I had been greatly looking forward to Raymond Ford's fortieth birthday party at the Conservative Club as a bit of light relief. Now I would have to miss it and all for the sake of collecting Caroline from her bloody piano lesson. Bugger, Bugger, Bugger!

Friday April 18th
Rang Raymond to apologise that I would not be able to attend his party after all because of Caroline's piano lesson. He said I should come along anyway even if it was late, which was kind of him.

While on the subject of Raymond, I heard today from a customer that he had opened yet another office, this time in the new shopping mall ... must be his fourth in the area. He's probably the most successful local estate agent – obviously very good at networking – or back-scratching as we used to call it. Not that I, or anyone I knew, really liked Raymond very much, and he was certainly not, I felt sure, the sort of person who would appeal to Marcia and her circle of middle-class liberal friends. 'Not quite the ticket' as my old friend Leonard once put it. A trifle snobbish perhaps but Raymond is undeniably rather flash and full of himself – none of which prevented any of us, of course, from accepting the invitation to his party!

I finally managed very late to reach the Conservative Club where Raymond's party was taking place. Winston Churchill looked down at me from his portrait above the mantelpiece in the main Club Room. 'What kept you, Old Cock?' he seemed to be saying. The Bollinger had finished, naturally, and all that was left was some lukewarm Chilean Chardonnay, a few congealed canapés and some other small eats. Some of the guests were already beginning to drift away. I stayed just long enough to wish Raymond a Happy Birthday before disconsolately driving home.

Life is no better than a cold cocktail sausage, I sometimes think!

Saturday 19th April

I've been having a truly dismal time recently, of which the dropping of The Pickwick Papers and the debacle over Raymond's party this week are only the latest of my woes. Last week, I managed to spill coffee on a valuable copy of Rob Roy, my car has been broken into twice in a month, vandals have smashed one of the shop windows, the radiator in the bathroom is leaking, I've had numerous silly rows with Marcia and this morning I had a shouting match with Caroline who seems lately to have become even more indolent and insolent than usual. On top of it all, my piles are playing me up again.

Almost as soon as I opened up the shop, the telephone rang. To my surprise, it was Raymond. He thanked me profusely for coming to his party and I thanked him in return and apologised for my late arrival.

"Martin, old scout," he said, "I hope you won't mind me saying but you were looking a bit stressed out last night'. Well, I did mind him saying – none of his business – and I wish he wouldn't call me 'old scout'. "In fact," he continued, "you've looked stressed for some time now. All the chaps at the pub have been saying the same thing. What you need is a break, on your own, away from it all, to chill out, re-charge the old batteries et cetera."

I murmured agreement, hoping that would put an end to the conversation, but he went on: "Martin, I've got a proposal: you could go and stay at my villa in Cyprus, it's free at the moment. Well, actually, it's not really my villa. I'm sort of warehousing it for a pal of mine who got in a spot of bother recently and needed to get it off balance sheet a bit sharpish. But it's alright, he won't mind if you use it, not at all."

"I see," I said. 'Well, it's very kind of you, Raymond. I shall have to think about it." It was quite absurd, of course. How could I possibly get away?

Sunday 20th April
Day of rest, I don't think! Having mown the lawn, Marcia suggested that I should take the car to the carwash at our local garage. I hadn't noticed that one of the windows was slightly open. The front passenger seat got saturated including a nice scarf which Marcia had given me for my birthday and the copy of the Sunday Times which I had just bought. If that were not enough, later I knocked over a bottle of red wine intended for our lunch, and, in the course of clearing up the mess, I had contrived to drop my phone in the kitchen sink which was full of water. Bugger, Bugger, Bugger!

Frankly, I was not even going to mention Raymond's offer of the villa in Cyprus, but the subject of holidays came up during lunch so I did, more as a joke than anything else. To my absolute amazement, far from laughingly dismissing the thing out of hand, Marcia actually thought that it was a good idea.

"Why not, Martin?" she said. "It would do you good to have a break – and me as well. Perhaps we need a rest from each other. For God's sake go, and come back when you feel less grumpy about everything."

Monday 21st April
I phoned Raymond at his office as soon as I arrived at the shop. The villa was still available and I accepted his kind offer. Marcia phoned me later

in the morning to say that she had booked me onto a cheap flight on the Internet, leaving this Saturday, the 26th. I met Alan Elworthy, a local bookbinder friend of mine, for lunch and he kindly agreed to look after the shop in my absence. And so, it was all arranged.

Actually, I'm quite looking forward to it.

Tom suggested we skip the next few entries which, at a cursory look, seemed to deal with a row with the garage about repairs to the car, frustration with the plumber who had failed to turn up when he said he would to mend the leaking radiator, and the insurers being awkward about the cost of the new shop window. Instead, we went straight to the day of Martin's departure for Cyprus.

Saturday 26th April

Ghastly queue for baggage drop at Luton, ghastly delay, long tedious flight, chaos in the baggage hall at Larnaca, ghastly ride on bumpy roads in very old taxi to Raymond's villa. This has all been a ghastly mistake. I shall go home tomorrow.

Sunday 27th April

Feeling better this morning after long sleep. Raymond's villa is designed and furnished in what I can only describe as the 'Costa Croydon' style. However, it is comfortable and has every possible modern convenience, including a small car available for my use. The view from the sun terrace is spectacular – sea in one direction, with a charming rocky cove just below the villa. Looking the other way, inland, lemon and olive groves compete with terraced vineyards climbing up the steep hillsides. A few donkeys, goats and peasants meander about. Most atmospheric! Perhaps I shall stay till next week.

Monday 28th April

Except for lunch at beachside taverna, spent day lounging about, splashing in the pool and reading. Very relaxing!

Tuesday 29th April

Visited Hotel Poseidon at Galypsos, my nearest town, where Raymond advised me the British community congregate. Very motley lot — a smattering of traditional ex-pat types who play bridge, drink gin fizzes and swear that they'll never go back to the UK unless capital gains tax is abolished, a dreary little man who used to run an industrial cleaning business in the Midlands and his mousy wife, a camp Liverpudlian who owns a boutique in the town, and a pair of elderly Scottish spinsters, former school-teachers from Glasgow, of whom everyone is absolutely terrified.

The main group, though, comprises a bunch of businessmen from north London who seem to commute regularly between Cyprus and Britain. They are all complete spivs of course, caricatures of themselves! They really do wear gold bracelets, medallions, and mobile phones in diamond-studded holders clipped to the waistband of their shorts. Extraordinary! Moreover, they all appear to know Raymond well, and because I'm staying at his villa, they think I must be one of their own. They simply will not accept that I run an antiquarian bookshop and assume that it is a front for something else. "I know what you sells," one of them said to me, tapping his nose, "it's 'ard core porn, init?" I shall avoid the Poseidon in future.

Wednesday 30th April

Found good restaurant at a village a mile inland called the Troodos, run by charming couple, Spiro and Melina. Superb lunch in pleasing ambience. Afternoon sleep.

Thursday 1st May

Another relaxing day spent largely on the sun terrace. Read a chapter or two of a novel I'd bought at the airport. Stavros the local farmer, goatherd and odd-job man came to clean the pool. He brought some disgusting local wine of his own making which I had to pretend to enjoy. Glorious sunset!

Tom suggested we skip forward again as many of the entries following the 1st of May were very short. One read simply read 'Booze and snooze'. He resumed again on the 20th of May.

Tuesday 20th May

Incredible! Have been here over three weeks already. Life is worth getting out of bed for after all! Life is a cloudless blue sky, the excitement and energy of a Greek dance, the joy of a dolphin leaping and pirouetting through the limpid waters of the bay! If my diary sounds like a handout from the local tourist office, I make no apology.

Wednesday 21st May

Wonderful meze at the Troodos where I'm quite a regular now. Melina, who is an absolute sweetie, gives me a big kiss and serves me a Greek brandy on the house.

Thursday 22nd May

Invited by one of the spivs to drinks on his giant motor cruiser, inevitably like a floating version of one of those mega-pubs. We are joined by some mafia types and a trio of splendidly tarty young woman wearing practically non-existent swimwear. I must confess I rather enjoyed myself, but relieved to return to the quiet of the villa.

Friday 23rd May

I recline on the sun lounger sipping a dry Martini cocktail. Occasionally I bestir myself enough to flop in the pool, replenish my glass or wave to Stavros in the distance as he tends his olive trees. Mostly though I simply lie there gazing at the incomparable view: the starkly beautiful coastline, the gentle swell lapping against the rocks below, and the brightly painted boats of the fishing fleet as they make their slow progress back to port over the 'wine dark sea'. I have obviously attained a state of Nirvana!

Again, Tom decided to miss out some of the following entries which continued in much the same ecstatic vein as that for the 23rd of May.

Monday 9th June

Something is wrong. This Nirvana business is not all it's cracked up to be. I think I must be suffering from 'perfection fatigue'. Life has suddenly become bland, boring, unreal. It is time to re-join the Real World. I want to go home. I want to experience the whiff of old books again. I want to hear the patter of raindrops. I even want to help Caroline with her holiday project on Emily Bronte and take her to piano lessons. I want to mow the lawn. I wouldn't even mind emptying the dishwasher occasionally. Most of all, I want to see Marcia. I shall go to the travel agent in Galypsos and book a flight.

Tuesday 10th June

Booked flight. Amazingly there was some availability on a flight tomorrow, Wednesday. A bit expensive but I decided to take it, otherwise I would have had to wait for another five days. Had final lunch at the Troodos and said 'goodbye' to Spiro and Melina – rather sad. Stavros came round in the evening to wish me farewell and insisted on sharing a bottle of his disgusting wine with me.

Wednesday 11th June

The taxi pulled up outside my house at about 10pm. It was later than I had anticipated, but I was home. The journey had been quite as long and tedious as the journey out, but, in my more equable frame of mind, I was able to withstand it better. I began to walk up the driveway towards the front door. The ground floor of the house was in darkness but there was a light on in our bedroom. Marcia must have gone to bed early. The window was open and the curtains were not drawn. It was a warmish evening.

I was about half way up the drive when Marcia herself appeared at the window, dressed in a very sexy black nightdress which I had not seen before. She looked absolutely ravishing, radiant, as beautiful as the day we married, a new woman! I wanted to cry out 'Marcia, I love you, I want you. Let's celebrate the start of our new life together' but of course I didn't. Marcia had obviously not seen me. She seemed to be staring dreamily into the middle distance. Quite suddenly she tossed back her head laughing and drew the curtains shut with a theatrical flourish.

So absorbed had I been in watching Marcia that it was only then that I
noticed the car parked near the garage. It was not one of ours. It was a
sleek black expensive-looking sports saloon and emblazoned on its side
in jazzy silver lettering were the words:

Make a fast move with Raymond Ford –
your friendly local estate agent.

FOUR

Rumours

I was at home going through the morning's post when Tom phoned. He asked if I could meet for lunch at the Prince of Denmark by the harbour. He'd asked Desmond to come along too. There was something he wanted to tell us. It was important, he said, but he didn't want to talk about it on the phone. *Odd*, I thought, but I agreed to be there.

The Prince of Denmark was crowded with holidaymakers at lunchtime, as it normally is, but I found that Tom and Desmond had already arrived and secured a table in one of the alcoves near the fireplace which offer a bit of privacy.

"Sorry to sound so mysterious about all this," Tom said, "but it's about the Colonel – I couldn't talk about it in the bar this evening hence asking you both to come here. It was something Commander Craddock saw."

"Commander Craddock?" Desmond asked.

"Yes, you know, Bob Craddock, president of the Sailing Club – comes in the Sloop quite often on a Friday."

"Yes, yes."

"Well," Tom continued. "Craddock was on his way home from the sailing club a couple of days ago and his route takes him passed the Colonel's house. Just as he was approaching, who should come out of the Colonel's front door but Emily? And as she went down the front path she turned and blew the Colonel a kiss."

"Emily?"

"Come on, wake up! Our Emily, at the Sloop – at least he thought it was her – Craddock was a little way off and, of course, he's been in the bar only once or twice since she started."

"You're surely not suggesting there's anything going on between them?" I said.

"Well, it's a bit odd, isn't it?"

"But there could be any number of explanations … from what you say Craddock was not even sure it was Emily."

"No, he was a little way up the road when he saw her. But, George, how many pretty young women do you think there are in Bufferton who might look like Emily?"

"Well, there's that nice Polish girl, Magda, at the chemists in Chapel Street. I know the Colonel has his prescriptions delivered. Magda might have been dropping off the Colonel's beta-blockers – at a distance she could easily have been taken for Emily."

"Yes, but would Magda blow the Colonel a kiss?"

"Do you know what?" Desmond chimed in, "come to think of it – and it might be just a coincidence – but I thought I saw the Colonel this morning walking along the front near the beach huts in the company of a young lady, who might have been Emily."

"You thought you saw him?" I said. "Are you sure? And what about the lady, can you be sure it was Emily?"

"Well, I couldn't say for sure. They were some way off, you see, and walking away in the opposite direction."

"Well, there you are then, both you and Commander Craddock could have been mistaken – and even if it was Emily coming out of the Colonel's house and it was the Colonel with Emily near the beach huts, it doesn't prove anything. The Colonel has always struck me as a man of principle and common sense. I can't see him allowing himself to get entangled with a young woman less than half his age. That sort of thing almost invariably ends in tears."

"What about that bloke with the Russian bride?" Tom said.

"Good point!" Desmond interjected.

"And let's not forget," Tom added pointedly, "that the Colonel is still good-looking, fit for a chap of his age and – even more to the point – he's a very wealthy man and a bachelor too!"

"You're surely not suggesting that Emily's a gold-digger, are you?" I asked incredulously.

"I would agree that Emily seems on the surface to be far too nice a girl for that sort of thing, but we don't really know much about her, do we?"

"Well, I still think all this is a load of old nonsense," I said. "The Colonel, I repeat, is much too prudent and sensible a man to pursue an affair with a very young woman he barely knows, let alone fall into a trap where money's concerned."

"Mark my words, George," Tom said, "when infatuation comes in through the door, prudence and common sense go flying out of the window!"

"And," Desmond interjected, "the Colonel has an eye for the ladies. Look at the way he used to peep down Gloria's cleavage!"

"Well, you're a fine one to talk, Desmond." I said. "The Colonel may have enjoyed the occasional peep. *You* positively gawped!"

"I thought I saw a glint in his eye on Emily's first day as our new barmaid." Desmond said, ignoring my interruption. "In fact, he takes a good look at any attractive young woman who comes in the bar."

"And," Tom added, "do you remember he once took Gloria out to dinner at the Bufferton Sands?"

"Look," I said. "It was Gloria's birthday and that silly former boyfriend of hers had just dropped her. The Colonel felt sorry for her. It was a kind gesture to ask her for dinner. That's all. There's no evidence of any impropriety with Gloria, let alone Emily…"

"You lawyers and your evidence! What about instinct?" Said Desmond, rather tartly.

"If I were to adopt your crude instincts, Desmond," I replied,

"I'd probably conclude that old Monsignor Michael at your church was having affairs with a string of chorus girls. In any event, whatever you chaps may believe, there's nothing much we can do about it."

"Not at the moment, I agree," Tom said, "but we should keep our eyes peeled and our ears pinned back."

"Well, all right, if you think so," I said. "But the idea that the Colonel of all people is having an affair with young Emily is preposterous."

"Now, one more important thing, I should mention," Tom continued, "old Craddock is a good friend of the Colonel and obviously doesn't want to be held responsible for spreading rumours about him. He told his wife, Jean what he'd seen – or thought he'd seen – on the basis she wouldn't say a word to anybody. Well, Jean plays bridge with Cara and told her the story – in the strictest confidence, of course, and Cara told me about it over supper last night in, er, er, the strictest of confidence, too. So, what I've told you now also must be treated ... "

" ... in the strictest of confidence," I added helpfully, in as innocent a tone as I could muster.

"Precisely. In the strictest of confidence."

"Of course, of course," Desmond and I hastened to agree.

To be fair, I too had observed that the Colonel noticeably perked up in the presence of a pretty face and Emily certainly had one of those, but he was not alone in that and of course it meant nothing whatever in itself. Much more concrete proof, I thought, was needed.

FIVE

Harry's Secret

Tom, Desmond and I were at the bar as usual. It was only just past six o'clock and the Colonel had not yet arrived. We didn't have to wait long though. We could hear his booming voice as he approached.

A moment or two later, he entered the bar accompanied by a pleasant-looking man with whom he had, presumably, just been conversing.

"Met this fellow on the sea front," he boomed. "Wanted to know the way here, said he'd heard that the back bar at the Sloop was the best place in Bufferton for a quiet drink in civilised company.

"Quite right! Follow me," I said, "and here we are. I'm so sorry I've forgotten your name already."

"Charles," the pleasant-looking man said, and we all shook hands and introduced ourselves.

"I suppose," he said, "this is the place to come if you want to hear all the local gossip."

"Certainly not!" Tom said. "We leave that sort of thing to the ladies at the bridge club, but we do from time to time get strangers in here, chaps like you in fact, from all over the country, and on occasion, if they're disposed to be friendly and we offer them a drink, they might tell us a yarn. We always enjoy a good yarn here, particularly ones involving some scandal or dark secret."

"Hmm," Charles said, "I shouldn't really but, if you'd really like to hear it, I could tell you a story which involves a most extraordinary, if not dark, secret about a friend and neighbour of mine in

London who has sadly passed away, a famous writer of travel books, in fact. You may have heard of him and perhaps read one of his books – Harry Marsh."

"Oh, yes indeed I have," Tom said.

"So have I, as a matter of fact," I said.

"Good, good. But look, before I start, you must promise me that not a word will go any further than this bar."

"My dear chap," I said, "you may rest assured that everything you say here will be treated in the very strictest of confidence. Now, what would you like to drink?"

"Well then," he said, after I had bought him a pint of beer, "I suppose I should begin with the day of Harry's funeral, last year. I was in the midst of the throng of mourners who had just attended the funeral service in the crematorium chapel and we were shuffling our way back along the short pathway towards the main road.

"Look, there goes poor Harry!" someone remarked, as the crematorium chimney emitted a little puff of grey smoke which soon merged with the gloomy October sky and disappeared.

One wonders whether it was in fact smoke from the incineration of Harry's remains or those of some other poor wretch whose funeral had taken place earlier that morning. Who can say? It didn't really matter, but the remark, a little tasteless though it seemed at the time, did somehow manage to underline Harry's own pragmatic view of the relative insignificance of our lives in the great scheme of things. Indeed, I recall him once saying *Charles, old boy, half the misery in the world could be avoided if only people didn't take themselves so damn seriously.*

Some of our number, it must be admitted, muttered disapprovingly at the puff of smoke remark, but others were unable to resist a little chuckle. I have to admit that I was one of the chucklers and I'm quite sure dear old Harry would have been one too.

Harry was a neighbour of mine in London. We both owned flats in the same building. Harry had lived there many years and I bought my own flat a good ten years ago. We became firm friends, and although he was often away for quite long periods, he always made a point of contacting me whenever he was at home there, and we would go out for lunch or dinner somewhere. If we were both at home of an evening he would often invite me in for a glass or two of champagne and sometimes for supper – he was an exceptionally good cook. I cannot imagine a more generous host or a more congenial companion.

Harry used to be a journalist. Indeed, much of his career he spent as a foreign correspondent first in New York, then Paris and finally in Rome. In his mid-fifties, however, he gave it all up to become a travel writer. His books have always been very popular with the public. Indeed, in my humble opinion, Harry produced classics of the genre.

As I'm sure anyone who has read any of Harry's books would agree, he succeeds in writing evocatively about places and people without ever resorting to the sort of indulgent waffle which is the besetting sin of much travel literature. Whether he describes the enjoyment of a champagne cocktail at some fashionable haunt in Paris or New York, a stroll through the luxuriant gardens of some grand villa in Fiesole overlooking Florence in the valley below, or a climb up some remote pass in the Atlas Mountains of Morocco, it seems to me that he manages to capture the essence of place and occasion so well that you almost feel that you are there yourself.

Then, his books brim with the colourful characters whom he always seemed to meet on his travels and engage in conversation – conversations ranging over all sorts of topics from high culture to low politics, from the ghastliness of multi-storey car-parks to the delightfulness of hedgehogs, from restaurants for fine dining the world over down to where to find the best fish and chips in London – apparently a modest chippie near Bank tube station, where the fish is cooked to perfection in the lightest of crispy batter, the chips are slender and golden but never soggy and the whole lot comes beautifully wrapped up for you to take away in pages of the *Financial Times*.

He was truly, in my view, the master of the well-crafted phrase – sharp, witty and engaging.

Harry died at his flat at the age of 75, a great deal older than me, but not old by today's standards. He was found by his cleaner one morning having, as the post mortem disclosed, suffered a massive heart attack during the night. I learnt of his death on my return home from work and I must say it came as a great shock to me. He had just returned home after one of his long absences, and we had had lunch together only a few days before he died. His demeanour then was as sprightly as always and he seemed fit and well. He had a phenomenal work rate, producing a new book every other year, and with sound commercial judgement he usually contrived to time their publication to coincide with the run-up to Christmas.

It was at his club in Pall Mall later on the day of his funeral that the wake took place. It was a very grand affair generously organised and paid for by his publisher and attended by a large gathering of the Great and the Good, leavened by a less respectable, but more amusing, smattering of the Small and Not So Good – such was the wide and varied circle of Harry's friends and admirers. No expense was spared – a seemingly endless supply of champagne fizzed and flowed and tray after tray of delicious canapés circulated with clockwork regularity.

Finally, though, the food and drink began to peter out and it was obviously time to go. However, as I was making my way out of the room, I caught sight of a woman who seemed somehow vaguely familiar. Possibly I had noticed her at the crematorium, but I felt sure that I had also seen her somewhere else before. Then, as these things sometimes do, it clicked into place. She was pictured in a photograph on a side table in Harry's flat. Obviously, I thought, this must be his niece, Alice, his only surviving relative, the daughter of his older brother. He had often talked about her and was plainly fond of her.

I decided it would be only right to offer my condolences on the death of her uncle and perhaps say a few words about how much I had valued his friendship. I tried to fight my way back in her direction, but she was lost to view in the crush of people and, by the time I got to where I'd seen her, she had gone.

Later that evening, the uplifting effect of the champagne finally wore off, leaving me feeling a little deflated, and as I prepared to go to bed, I recalled the tiny puff of smoke from the crematorium chimney and a sudden overwhelming sense of sadness overcame me ... sadness that I should never see poor Harry again; never again enjoy one of those jolly lunches and dinners with him to which I so looked forward; never sip a glass or two of champagne at his flat; never again hear his cheerful laugh. "Farewell, Harry!" I muttered to myself. "Farewell, I shall miss you, miss you very much indeed."

Harry was a bachelor and I had never heard him even mention a woman, except for his niece. I am single too but I was married once. My wife left me for another man – my fault entirely as I spent too much time at work auditing accounts, calculating tax liabilities, and helping to draft business plans. Yes! You'll have guessed – I'm an accountant. Not a bad job on the whole, despite what some people may say. But as with any other walk of life there is a danger of falling into a rut. Larger than life people like Harry, help us all to adopt a wider perspective on the world. During the dark autumn months, life diggered on as life does and I often thought of Harry, particularly when arriving late home after another tedious day at the office. Sometimes, I even forgot that he was no longer with us and fondly imagined that he would soon return from some foreign adventure and I would bump into him on the stairs.

Often Harry and I spent Christmas Day together. He did the cooking and I provided the wine, but what was I to do for Christmas after his death? I certainly didn't fancy spending it all alone in my flat. By chance, I saw an advertisement in a magazine in the doctor's waiting room offering a 'Gourmet Christmas break' here at the Bufferton Sands Hotel. They had one single room left when I telephoned, and I took it.

Good decision! There were some jolly people staying at the hotel and seeing that I was on my own, they invited me to join their table for the Christmas lunch and I spent what was left of the day in a pleasant alcoholic haze. On Boxing Day, I felt the need for an invigorating walk, and on the advice of the hotel receptionist, I decided to walk along the headland to Gull Point and back. As you will know, there are two ways to Gull Point, the public footpath along the ridge of the headland and a lane at a lower level which is more sheltered. It was a bright but breezy day and I opted fortuitously for the more sheltered route. It is a lovely walk with the bay on one side and isolated cottages and seaside villas on the other. About halfway along, I came upon a most attractive regency guesthouse called Gull View, clad in slate tiles with pale blue window shutters and set in a large well-kept garden. Perhaps you know it? I stood for a few moments admiring the place and I was just about to walk on when a woman emerged from a small woodshed carrying logs for the fire. I recognised her instantly. It was the woman I'd seen at Harry's wake, the woman in the photograph on the side table in his flat.

"Hello," I said, "are you by chance Harry Marsh's niece Alice?"

She was, she said, a little surprised, and asked if we'd met before.

I explained who I was, my connection with Harry and how I came to believe that she was his niece.

So, she invited me in have a nice cup of tea.

I helped her in with the logs, she made a pot of tea and we sat together in front of the fire. She was a little coy at first, but she soon opened up and what an extraordinary tale she had to tell!

Her father, Harry's older brother Jeremy, was a barrister but he suffered from chronic ill-health. Eventually, in his early fifties, the strains and stresses of life at the bar became too much for him and he retired. A short while later, he and his wife moved down to Devon and bought Gull View. It was thought that the fresh sea air would do him good. To supplement their income, Gull View was converted into a guesthouse. Alice's mother, who was much younger and fitter, did most of the work, of course, while her father entertained the guests with stories of courtroom dramas and anecdotes about witty judges and eccentric barristers.

Sadly, a few years later, Jeremy's health deteriorated. He suffered a stroke and died a few weeks later. This all happened when Alice was still a student, studying at university. Naturally, Harry came down for the funeral and stayed at the guesthouse. It was around this time, too, that Harry retired from journalism and began his second career as a travel writer.

About a month after the funeral, Alice came home to Gull View from university for the weekend and was surprised to find Harry still there. She immediately suspected that he was having an affair with her mother. But that wasn't the case at all. Harry was fond of her mother but wasn't in love with her or having an affair. It was Gull View that he had fallen in love with: the peace, the glorious coastal views and the wonderful sound of the waves crashing against the rocks below. It was with reluctance that he returned to London, vowing to return as soon as he could.

Some six months later, however, the mother accepted a proposal of marriage from a businessman from Guildford who had also recently lost his spouse. He had been one of the regular guests at Gull View, a kind man and apparently a wealthy one too. Alice was pleased for her mother, who might now have the chance of an easier life, but feared that Gull View would be sold and possibly revert to its former use as a private house. She was surprised, therefore, when her mother offered to transfer it into her name if she agreed to continue to run it as a guesthouse. Whether the mother couldn't bear to sell it or possibly wanted the property and business kept in the family as an insurance against her new marriage not working out, it was difficult to say.

Accepting her mother's offer would mean giving up university and running a B&B, not exactly the career option she had in mind. Nevertheless, bravely, that's what she decided to do. It was tough going at first for one so young and inexperienced, but she had the support of an older lady from Bufferton whom her mother had employed part-time and who understood the business. As a most attractive young woman, Alice had several boyfriends over the years but never married, presumably because of her overriding commitment to Gull View and the business.

Not long after Alice took over Gull View and her mother's remarriage, something else happened which was entirely unexpected – she received a letter from Harry with a most surprising proposal: he would like to reserve a room in the B&B for his exclusive use and for which he would be prepared to pay an annual rent up-front. He wished, he said, to spend as much time at Gull View as possible.

I found this quite extraordinary, of course. How on earth, I wondered, could Harry, as a travel writer, afford to spend any time in Devon while keeping up what must have been a very busy schedule travelling to all corners of the globe?

I asked Alice to explain.

Alice replied that Harry didn't travel round the globe He didn't go anywhere else after he retired as a journalist. His only journeys were from London to Gull View by train via Exeter where Alice normally picked him up by car from the station.

This was utterly mystifying.

I couldn't understand. What about all those wonderful descriptions of cities, palaces, cathedrals, mosques, mountains, jungles, rivers?

As Alice observed, Harry's experiences as a foreign correspondent, at least in those places where he was based, would no doubt have helped, but chasing international news stories is not the same as travelling for pleasure or cultural interest. It does not automatically take you to the same destinations or places of note, let alone the hidden gems and forgotten corners of the world which travel writers like to write about. Some descriptions of places were clearly based on his memories as a foreign correspondent or his life in London, but many more descriptions in his travel books were based simply on meticulous research. He possessed an extensive collection of travel literature and books about art, architecture, history and culture, which he kept at Gull View, and of course when he was in London, he would visit libraries if more information was needed.

Still unable quite to believe all this, I asked about the journeys which are the core of his books, the extraordinary adventures and experiences he had and which he wrote about so vividly.

Most were inventions of his creative mind, she told me.

"And what about all those extraordinary people he met and talked to?" I asked.

"As often as not, wonderful figments of his lively imagination," she assured me.

"Good God!" I exclaimed.

Alice smiled. The fact was, she told me, that, as a journalist and foreign correspondent, Harry had spent long periods away from home. He had grown tired of the tedious business of travelling, of the feeling of not truly belonging anywhere. He missed England, his London club and his friends.

That was the reason, Alice explained, why he had given up his job. Harry enjoyed life in London, but he loved Gull View even more, and this is where he liked to spend much of his time and where he did the bulk of his research and all of his writing.

The big secret about Harry was that he was the travel writer who never travelled.

SIX

Posh Tart

My brother, Marcus, was down for the weekend. He lives in London but visits Bufferton from time to time and I spend the odd weekend with him at his flat up in London. Unlike me, Marcus still works more or less full time and I don't think he'll give it up. He is a bachelor and a gregarious fellow by nature. His business involves travel and contact with all sorts of different people, and he plainly enjoys the life far too much ever to consider retirement.

He calls himself an export/import agent. I've never been too sure what this entails but he certainly seems to make a lot of money at it. My wife Molly doesn't much care for Marcus and considers him a bit of a rogue. I cannot speak for his business dealings but I must admit this is certainly true as far as his relationships with women are concerned. To avoid family friction, Marcus generally stays at the Bufferton Sands Hotel when he comes to visit, and he always makes a point of joining Tom, Desmond, the Colonel and me at the Sloop for a drink on the evening of his arrival.

"Hello, chaps!" Marcus greeted us, as he sauntered in. "Very good to see you all again – but where's the lovely Gloria?"

"Gone to work in Exeter, I'm afraid," Tom said.

"Dear me, that's a shame, but this new girl behind the bar is jolly tasty, though, isn't she?!" He said, lowering his voice to a whisper. "Do you think she'd like to come out to dinner with me one evening?"

"No, I jolly well don't," I said firmly. "You're far too old, ugly and wicked and she's far too young, pretty and nice."

"Oh, that's a pity!"

"By the way," Tom said, changing the subject, "how do you like the Bufferton Sands now it's been all been tarted up?"

"Well, actually, I'm not staying there this time. My finances are a bit wobbly at present, so I'm up at a little B&B near the old church."

"Why's that?" I asked.

"Earlier this year I made a very expensive investment which exhausted most of my available cash resources, and it's going to take a few more deals to replenish the coffers."

"What sort of investment?"

"Well, a quite unusual one, or rather one where the prospective return was, er, let us say, of an unconventional nature."

"Really?"

"Oh, dear, I suppose I shall have to come clean and tell all, otherwise you'll go on nagging me forever."

"Go on, then," said the Colonel. "Sounds intriguing."

WELL, I WAS LUNCHING ONE DAY at a favourite haunt of mine. While waiting to place my order, I was enjoying a pre-prandial drink at the bar and there was this woman leaning on the counter, gazing wistfully up at the ceiling. She'd finished her drink but obviously wasn't in any hurry to order another.

She saw me looking at her and smiled. Well, of course, I knew straightaway precisely what she was, despite the sophisticated appearance and smart designer clothes – a posh tart! I've had a lifetime's experience of meeting women in bars and I've seen that distinctive smile a thousand times. I sidled casually over to her and asked if she'd like a drink. Yes, she'd have a Kir Royale. Two drinks later, we were having a cosy lunch together in the restaurant. Two hours later, we were in bed at her flat. No ordinary tart's parlour either, I should add, not large, but very cosy and charming, most tasteful and civilised, too – all Turkish rugs, Georgian tallboys and Mozart CDs.

Samantha was her name. Absolutely ravishing female! Look, here's a photo, gives you some idea – doesn't do her justice, though. And as for the sex ... well, let's just say that her fee, though three times as much as I've ever paid for that sort of service anywhere else, represented superb value – every whim indulged, every fancy catered for, full English breakfast included. And she offered me a discount, too, if I became a regular punter. I was hooked, of course!

There was one thing that puzzled me about Samantha, though. She was a bit too classy even for a posh tart or an upmarket call girl.

All became clear next morning, when she told me her story. She'd married this bloke Henry Roberts, believing that he was a very wealthy businessman. They had enjoyed a lavish life-style and all seemed hunky-dory. Then about two years ago Henry was killed in a skiing accident and everything began to unravel. It transpired that he was effectively, well, a fraudster, a conman. Worse still, apparently, he'd persuaded her to invest the bulk of her family inheritance in some business enterprise which turned out to be completely fictitious – simply a front for channelling funds into his private bank account to be frittered away on extravagant living. Henry's only real asset was his undoubted charm. All the money had virtually disappeared, of course. It was fortunate, she said, that the flat was in her name, but there was a substantial mortgage and a child at an expensive prep school in Berkshire. This was why she'd decided to go on the game, as women of that profession call it. With practically no money left, how else could she maintain her lifestyle and pay for the child's education?

Well, I saw a lot of Samantha over the following weeks. If I wasn't at work, asleep or pissed, I was positively overwhelmed with desire, I can tell you!

Then, one evening when I called, I found her in tears. The bank had called in the mortgage on the flat, and was threatening to foreclose. She had tried to find alternative finance, but without success. Could I help?

What did she suggest, I asked?

Well, perhaps I would like to buy the flat for the amount of the outstanding mortgage debt of £350,000 but then let her stay there on an informal basis? She trusted me to look after her and she would pay for her continued occupation by providing her personal services for free.

Well, of course, I jumped at the idea. I reckoned the flat was worth at least half a million on the open market, and then of course there were those delightful *personal services* whenever I desired. I even offered to help a bit with the school fees so she could come off *the game* and take a regular job. I wanted to be her only client you see, have her all to myself.

She said that she would contact her solicitor as soon as possible. I would also need a solicitor, of course, to represent my interests but rather than use my own regular bloke she suggested that I consider appointing the solicitor who had acted for the lady who had recently purchased the flat above hers. She didn't know him herself but the lady concerned, with whom she was on friendly terms, had been full of praise for the quick and efficient manner in which he had handled her purchase. The advantage was that he would already be familiar with the legal setup, which would obviously be common to all the flats in the block, and this would surely help to speed matters along. I agreed that this seemed like a good idea and Samantha said that she would find out his name and contact number. The next morning Samantha emailed me with the details and I duly phoned the chap up. He readily agreed to act for me and assured me that he would immediately make contact with Samantha's solicitor to set the wheels in motion.

Some while later, this solicitor fellow, a bright young man in a smart suit with a well-trimmed moustache, called at my office by appointment. He told me that the legal side of things was all in order and that, in the interests of speed and because Samantha trusted me as a friend, it had been agreed with her solicitor to dispense with a formal contract and proceed straight to completion of the deal, thus enabling the discharge of Samantha's mortgage and the transfer of the flat into my name with greater expedition. I signed some document or other and agreed to arrange for my bank to transfer to him a sum equal to the purchase price, stamp duty and legal costs in accordance with a statement which he produced. In anticipation, I had already arranged a substantial transfer of funds from my savings to my current account which was sufficient to cover the amount involved. Subject to receipt of the money, the fellow advised that completion of the purchase would take place exactly a week later.

I happened to be in Brussels on business the day completion was due to occur, but managed to speak to the solicitor bloke on his mobile and he had confirmed that the transaction had duly gone through. I flew back to Heathrow that very evening. On my arrival, I felt a desperate urge for a personal service so, joining the queue for passport control, I phoned Samantha on her home number. There was no reply; I tried her mobile and this time she answered.

"It's me Marcus, your *Seigneur* urgently requiring a bit of *droit*!" I said. "Are you at home now? I phoned your landline just now but there was no answer."

"Sorry," she said, "I didn't hear. I've just this second come out of the shower."

I could visualise her lovely naked body, all warm, wet and glistening.

"Well, don't bother to put any clothes on, darling. Just wrap yourself in a towel or something. I'll be with you in two shakes of a dog's tail!"

"See you soon then, you dirty dog!" she said, with a throaty chuckle.

Well, you can imagine I was in a rare fever of excitement as the taxi deposited me outside St. Matthews Court where Samantha lived. I bounded up to the front door of the block and pressed the entry phone button for her flat, or rather now my flat. There was no reply, so I tried again – still no reply.

I stood there, a little nonplussed, and was about to phone Samantha again on the mobile when a man came up behind me.

"Can I help you?" He said, "I live here."

I asked if he could let me in. I said I'd come to see Mrs. Roberts, but that there was no reply, although I knew she was there. Perhaps, I suggested, the bell was faulty?

He said he wasn't aware of anyone called Mrs Roberts.

But surely, I protested, he must know Samantha Roberts the owner, or rather former owner, of Flat 4. I said that the flat now actually belonged to me, though Samantha was staying on there. I had only recently, I told him, completed the purchase and didn't yet have a key of my own.

He replied that of course he knew Samantha in Flat 4, but she was a Miss Harper, and she'd never been the owner. All the residents, he said, were just tenants. The landlord was a private company, J.S. Brook Investments, which owned the whole block and let the flats out on short tenancies. In any case, he told me, Samantha certainly wasn't there now. The flat was empty. A new tenant was due to move in at the weekend. Miss Harper had moved out a few days ago. A removal van had come to collect all her stuff and afterwards she was seen leaving in a taxi in the company of a smart young man with a moustache.

Flight to Paradise cancelled and no refund! Naturally, I *never suspected* a thing…

SEVEN

Nelson and Emma

Sometimes we sit at a table, sometimes on stools at the bar. All but one stool. That one is reserved for Nelson.

Nelson is the pub cat. Nobody knows quite where he came from. He just arrived in the bar one day and decided that's where he wanted to make his home. He goes off somewhere during the daytime, but always returns each evening. The landlord's wife dotes upon him and, being a cat, of course he has very much exerted his authority over the house.

At first none of us noticed the chap who came into the bar and perched himself on a stool. He was not a regular and, poor chap, he couldn't have been expected to know it wasn't his to sit on.

It wasn't long before Nelson made his appearance from wherever he'd been. He was plainly miffed that his precious place had been taken and lost no time in strutting over to sit at the foot of the stool and stare malevolently at the usurper.

It didn't take long for the usurper to notice.

"I can see that I have committed a grave social error," he said.

"Well, not your fault at all. How would you possibly have known that you had taken Nelson's place?" Tom replied in a conciliatory tone. "Nelson's the pub cat, you know. He always sits there. However, there's a stool for you over here, next to George."

I duly smiled at the mention of my name and with a polite gesture indicated the empty stool beside me.

The stranger, plainly a good egg, seemed to grasp the situation perfectly. He promptly evacuated Nelson's stool and made his way to the free one next to me.

"Interesting coincidence that your pub cat is called Nelson."

"Why's that?" I asked.

"Well, I have a cat called Emma, and Nelson's mistress was, of course, Emma Hamilton."

"You'd better not bring her here then. We wouldn't want any impropriety of that sort in Bufferton!" Tom said, affecting a theatrical look of disapproval.

"No chance of that," our visitor replied. "Emma's being waited upon hand and foot by my neighbours in London in my absence, her every whim and fancy catered for. Emma's a thoroughbred Persian cat, a most aristocratic creature, quite unlike Emma Hamilton who, I believe, began life as a maid and later worked as a dancer and actress – even if later she became Lady Hamilton. It would be no exaggeration to say that Emma, I mean the cat not the ghost of Lady Hamilton, forced me to change my life."

"You know," intoned the Colonel who had been unusually quiet until then. "I feel a story coming on. You really must tell us all just how this imperious beast managed to alter your life and quite in what manner."

"Yes, yes, please." The rest of us chorused.

"Well," began our visitor "If you insist…"

"We do," I said, and I introduced myself and the others to this rather charming fellow.

"And my name's Gregory Todman," he said, "and I hope you won't find my story too silly!"

"I'm sure, we won't," I said.

"Because it is a rather silly story, but there it is. Well, here goes."

SOME YEARS AGO, MY WIFE Hazel left me for a man called Fairweather, an antiques dealer, whom she met when he came to value an old bureau bookcase left to me in my uncle's will. He was a slick, smooth-talking sort of chap, rather smarmy I thought, but he certainly knew what he was about. I had no idea that following this visit he and my wife had embarked on an affair, until one day,when I returned home after lunch at my club and found a note on the hall table: she'd left me to start a new life with this smarmy bastard.

Anyway, the affair didn't last. She next went off with a French polisher bloke. I believe she must have met him through Fairweather. He probably had dealings with him in the antique business.

I gather incidentally that it is called 'French polishing' because the practice started in France in the nineteenth century where there was apparently a taste for highly polished surfaces on furniture. It so happened that this French polisher, for whom she dumped Fairweather, was French himself by the name of Francois Levine, a *French* French polisher in fact.

He was no humble artisan. I gathered that he came from an upper-class background, a once wealthy Parisian family that had fallen on hard times. He was apparently a well-educated man of a suave, refined appearance and, no doubt, oodles of Gallic charm. He had no money, however, and my wife eventually dumped him, too.

Despite everything, I still loved my wife and nurtured hopes that she would return to me. Indeed, when her affair with Levine broke up I truly believed that a reconciliation was on the cards, but it was not to be. Instead, my wife took up with an investment banker with an elegant apartment in Knightsbridge and asked for a divorce.

All this was very upsetting of course, and my life fell apart. I lost interest in things, standards slipped. My flat became an absolute mess. I never dusted or made any effort to tidy things up. It was as much as I could do to get up in the morning to go to work. Even my wonderful cleaning lady gave up on me and handed in her notice. She said she couldn't cope any longer with all the mess and muddle.

Some while later I received a surprise call from my Aunt Lucy in Hampshire. She was getting on years and not in the best of health. Rather reluctantly, she had decided to move into a care home. The problem was what to do with her beloved cat, Emma. Would I be prepared to take care of her?

Well, as you might imagine I was far from keen on the idea, but I was very fond of my aunt. While I was at boarding school, my parents lived abroad in Geneva where my father worked for the United Nations, and I had spent many of my holidays with her at her pretty cottage in the glorious Hampshire countryside. She was always very kind to me. I owed her ...

So, about a week later, on a Saturday afternoon, a few days before Aunt Lucy was due to move into the care home, I travelled down to Hampshire to pick up Emma and transport her to London, along with her basket, litter tray and a large bag of cat food. There was a tear in poor auntie's eye as she helped me get Emma into the car.

Aunt Lucy warned me that Emma was quite a determined cat, not one, as she put it, *to let I dare not wait upon I would* like Shakespeare's poor cat in the adage. Emma always knew exactly what she wanted, Auntie said, and wouldn't give up until she got it. I laughed, not knowing quite what to make of all this, but I was soon to find out.

It was late when I eventually arrived home, and having given Emma a handful of the cat food in case she was still hungry, I retired to bed.

Living on my own, sometimes on Sundays I didn't even bother to get dressed until lunchtime, and then only if I was going off to the pub.

Emma's first Sunday with me was no exception. I shambled into the kitchen in my old dressing gown. First, I remembered to feed Emma and to provide her with some water as my aunt had instructed. Next, I prepared for myself a humble breakfast of cornflakes, a mug of tea and a couple of slices of toast. Having cleared a space on the kitchen table – pushing away the congealed remains of an Indian takeaway – I sat down to eat.

I noticed that Emma, having nibbled a little of her food, had jumped onto the working top next to the kitchen sink, managing to find a space for herself beside a pile of dirty plates. I looked at her for a brief instant and she looked back at me with what seemed to me a cold stare of disapproval. I took no notice at first, but something made me look up at her again.

She stared back again with the same disdainful, disapproving look as before. It was somehow unsettling and made me feel quite uncomfortable.

I tried to ignore her, but all the time I was conscious of her looking at me and I couldn't help myself from looking back. On each occasion, I was accorded that same intense stare of disapproval. Aunt Lucy was always such a neat and tidy person, and Emma would have had nothing about which to complain. Plainly, however, I failed to live up to her high expectations.

I tried to persuade myself, without success, that I was being silly. But in the end I could stand it no longer. I got up from my chair and returned to the bedroom.

It didn't take me long to decide what I had to do. I swiftly donned my smart Italian blazer, grey flannel trousers, a clean blue shirt and the natty tie which I often wore when I wanted to impress someone. Of course, during the working week, I wore a business suit for work, but that was just a routine requirement like a soldier putting on his uniform. This was an entirely different matter. I looked at myself in the bedroom mirror in the smart outfit I'd just chosen to wear. That should satisfy the blasted cat, I thought!

After combing my untidy hair, I left the bedroom to return to the kitchen. Emma looked me up and down slowly. Then, seemingly quite satisfied, she jumped off from where she had been sitting and resumed her breakfast.

A second or two later, the most extraordinary thing happened. I experienced a sudden and extraordinary change of mood – I felt that I was myself again, my old self, I mean, my true self as I used to be in former times, not the poor self-pitying wretch I'd recently become.

Next, I surveyed the mess into which, shamefully, I'd allowed my flat to descend, and spent most of the rest of that Sunday clearing, dusting and generally tidying things up. By the time I'd finished the place was more or less restored to something like it used to be. Not perhaps in the same league as one of those perfect places featured in *House & Home* magazine, but it was a proper home again.

At work the next day, Monday, my secretary complimented me on my unusually cheery mood. And when I returned home that evening a warm feeling of contentment stole over me. I felt myself a happier person than I'd been for many a month.

Emma appeared, circling my legs and rubbing herself against me. She looked up at me, purring noisily, whiskers all perky. No disapproving stare this time, but a feline look of pure devotion.

I was about to open a bottle of wine and pour myself a celebratory glass, when the doorbell sounded. I opened the door to find a very attractive young lady holding a parcel, which she said had arrived for me from Amazon at lunchtime. It was a book I'd ordered some days before.

She told me that her name was Sophie Fisher and that she was the new tenant in the basement flat, just moved in that morning.

I thanked her for delivering the parcel, said it was a pleasure to meet her and hoped she'd be happy in her new home. As I spoke, I happened to notice Emma looking up at me and could swear that there was a glint in her eye.

Rather surprised at my own forwardness, I mentioned that I was just about to open a bottle of wine and wondered whether she would care for a glass.

She enthusiastically accepted my offer – and it was to be the start of something special.

I'm happy to say that Sophie and I are now engaged to be married just as soon as my divorce comes through. We're staying for the weekend at the Bufferton Sands Hotel, and I thought I'd just pop out for a drink while she had a facial at the beauty spa there. Indeed, I'm glad I did as I would not otherwise have enjoyed the pleasure of the company of you kind gentlemen, and I would like to thank you all for your patience in listening to my story.

Let me finish by paying tribute to Emma, a very special cat, to whom I entirely owe my salvation.

"Jolly good show!" The Colonel boomed heartily – a sentiment shared by us all.

EIGHT

Classic Cars

"My round. Same again, everyone?" Tom asked.

"Yes, same again." The Colonel replied in his deep, growly voice. "And me too, thanks Tom," Desmond added.

"Well," I said, "I ought really to be getting off home now. "Oh, come on, George. It's only just after seven. You've plenty of time."

"Well, all right then. Just a quick one."

∗∗∗

"Do you know that some folk here apparently refer to us as 'The Old Buffer Brigade' would you believe?" I said in a tone of disapproval. "I'm sure it's meant kindly but it's hardly a fair description, is it? After all, most of the other regulars at this bar are at least as old as we are."

"I must say I don't much like the expression Old Buffer," said Tom, "though I admit I may be an Old Codger."

"What's the bloody difference, for God's sake?" Desmond asked.

"Well," Tom explained "an Old Buffer is a chap of advanced years who may be of a genial disposition but has become a bit woolly-minded, while an Old Codger is an elderly bloke, often eccentric, but one who still has his wits about him."

"So, an Old Buffer is a sort of Colonel Blimp figure, you mean?" Desmond replied.

"More or less." Tom agreed.

"Here, steady on!" the Colonel barked loudly.

"Oh, you're not one of those blimpish types, Colonel … not at all!" Tom put in, hastily. "You're an Old Codger like the rest of us."

"I'm much obliged," the Colonel replied a bit huffily, only slightly mollified.

"I thought that the thing about Old Codgers is that they're always grumbling about something," I said. "In fact, the very word codger rather seems to chime with the word curmudgeon."

"You know," said Desmond, his mild Irish brogue somewhat accentuated. "I'd prefer to be a genial Old Buffer than a miserable old grumbler … surely a happier soul."

"Well, I disagree," said the Colonel. "I thoroughly enjoy grumbling – it doesn't make me miserable in the least. Nothing like a good grumble – does one a power of good!"

Tom and I hastened to agree with the Colonel but I hoped – and I could see from the slightly weary expression on his face that Tom was of like mind – that someone, anyone at all, might find a way to distract us from this rather fruitless discussion, preferably someone with a good story to tell.

And right on cue, someone did.

The someone was a man, whom we all knew, by the name of Derek Finch. Derek is not a resident of Bufferton Regis but lives and works in London. However, he keeps a boat at the local marina and, when he's down here, he invariably pops into our little bar for a chat and a drink.

"Hello chaps," he chipped in breezily, "Would you like to hear a funny story?"

Well, of course we did. As anyone who knows us will tell you, we're suckers for a good story, and I was rather glad that I'd decided to stay, risking the wrath of my wife for getting home late.

After Tom had bought him a drink, Derek settled himself on an empty stool and began his story:

It all started one Friday evening after work. As usual, I dropped into the local wine bar near my home in Chelsea. There were the usual gang of regulars there, John who's an accountant, Kenneth a civil engineer, Francis a solicitor – there's always a solicitor, isn't there? – and me, a publisher, as you know. Unlike you lot of old crusties down here, we're all still working, you know, and paying loads of tax to fund your pensions and healthcare!

We hadn't been there long that evening when a newcomer, a posh, snappily-dressed fellow, sailed in and asked if he might join us. Neither I nor the others could remember ever seeing him before, but we allowed him to pull up a chair to our table. He introduced himself as Roger Duffoy.

Despite a slightly pompous air, dovetailing with his posh appearance, he seemed, on first acquaintance, a perfectly friendly, likeable sort of fellow.

After half an hour or so and generously paying for a bottle of champagne, he got up to leave. He had a dinner engagement at the Dorchester he said and, in a stage whisper, a grand dinner for some national charity of which he was the current president. He promised, however, to be back for a drink with us later in the week.

And, after wishing us a cheery *bonne soirée* he was gone, turning briefly at the door to give us a little wave. We were all sitting at our usual table close to the window. I happened to look out and observed Roger as he crossed the road and approached a lovely vintage, maroon-coloured Bentley Continental in mint condition.

I called the other chaps to take a look as well.

We all peered out of the window and gasped as Roger lowered himself into the driver's seat and drove away.

I remember Francis saying that Roger had at least got some style, even if he was a bit flash, a view with which none of us could disagree. Obviously, it appeared that Roger was not short of a bob or two, we all thought.

***

Roger continued to be a quite frequent visitor, at least once a week, and indeed we had more or less accepted him as a regular though we wondered why he had chosen to frequent our little bar in particular. His explanation was that a favourite aunt of his lived very nearby, aged and sadly not in the best of health. Roger endeavoured, he said, to go and see her whenever he could. After these visits, he invariably felt the need for a drink and who could blame him. Our bar, he thought, looked a thoroughly civilised sort of place, where he believed he'd feel at home, and it was conveniently just across the road from where he usually parked his car.

Sometimes he was driving the Bentley and sometimes it was another classic – each one in perfect condition. Once, we saw him drive off in a priceless pre-war Bugatti Roadster of which I was deeply envious. Collecting classic cars was, so he told us, one of his greatest passions.

I must say he was entertaining company, though he did rather hog the conversation and spoke in a loud plummy voice, audible not just to those of us to whom he was speaking but across the whole bar. He seemed to know a great many famous people, from actors and film directors to well-known writers, politicians and others. It would only be a slight exaggeration to say that the bar reverberated to the sound of names being dropped, like ripe apples in an orchard on a blowy day.

The more we saw of him the more we gradually learnt about him. Indeed, he was more than forthcoming. His ancestors were apparently Huguenots, hence the French-sounding name, and like so many Huguenot families who had settled in England, they had done rather well for themselves over the centuries. He told us he lived in a large Edwardian mansion in Hampstead, of which he proudly showed us a picture on his phone.

He also confessed to owning several other properties across Europe – a spacious apartment in Paris overlooking the Champs de Mars, a ski chalet at Verbier in Switzerland and an enormous villa on the Costa Smeralda in Sardinia with its own private beach. Mouth-watering photos of all these delightful properties were flashed before us. If he had been anyone else, one might have considered this a rather vulgar way of showing off, the sort of thing a 'got-rich-quick' *parvenu* might do, but it was difficult to take exception to him; he was such a charmer – not to mention overwhelmingly generous. Invariably he would order a bottle of champagne, sometimes two, and refuse to accept any contribution towards the bill.

We all wondered what he did for a living to support such a lavish lifestyle. I hadn't liked to ask myself but Ken, originally a north-country lad, retains some of that blunt northern directness and had no such reservations. Roger, to do him justice, didn't seem to mind. He described himself as an *investor*. He had been lucky, he said, to have come into money under a family trust and had used a percentage of his wealth to invest in a variety of different concerns in the UK, Europe and America – investments from which he appeared to have prospered mightily.

I must say we all looked forward to Roger's visits to our bar, and used to take bets on which of his cars he would be driving.

Then one Saturday my wife and I were invited to the wedding in Sussex of the daughter of an old colleague of mine. It was a very grand affair. The marriage service itself took place in a lovely old medieval village church, and the reception was held at a country house hotel a few miles away.

It was a no-expense-spared reception – a delicious lunch at which the Champagne happily continued to flow all afternoon. I was glad we'd come down by train and had booked ourselves into the hotel for the night.

I hadn't seen the car in which the happy couple had been driven to the church – we were already seated in our pews – nor when the couple were driven from the church. However, when they left the reception the car, which no doubt had been parked somewhere nearby, duly drew up garlanded in ribbons to whisk them away. As I and the other guests cheered them off in traditional fashion, I got a good view of a maroon-coloured vintage Bentley Continental.

I was quite certain that it was the one that belonged to Roger Duffoy. Not only was it the same colour and vintage but it had all the same old motoring club badges. There was no doubt about it. I assumed that Roger must know the family and had kindly offered his precious vehicle for use as the wedding car. A bit strange, though, I thought, that he was not present himself on the occasion.

My old colleague and his wife, the parents of the bride, had also opted to stay the night at the hotel, and over a drink in the bar that evening, I mentioned the matter of the car.

I said that it was kind of Roger Duffoy to lend the use of his car for the wedding. He didn't know what I was talking about. He said that he'd arranged the car though a firm called Regency Hire, though added that the bloke he had dealt with, the sales manager of this outfit, was a Mr. Duffy.

Well, this was all too much of a coincidence. It seemed to me highly likely that Duffy and Duffoy were one and the same. I was not sure quite sure what to make of all this, but it appeared that our new friend Roger was not perhaps all that he had made himself out to be.

I couldn't wait to tell the story to the chaps at the wine bar.

***

"And what did your friends at the wine bar make of this extraordinary turn of events?" Tom enquired.

"They were as bemused as I was."

"Did you ever see this man Duffoy, or Duffy again?" The Colonel asked.

"No," Derek replied. "He never appeared at the wine bar again but about two months or so later Jimmy, the chief barman, came over to our table clutching a copy of the *Evening Standard*. He plonked the paper down on our table and, with a big wink, told us to take a look at page five where we would find an article that he was sure would be of great interest to us.

So, I put down my drink and took up the paper from the table, and duly turned to page five. There at the top of the page under the headline *The Cheating Caretaker,* were two pictures. I held up the paper for the others to see. One of pictures showed a row of classic cars, many of which we recognised, and the other one was of Roger Duffoy – or Duffy as we now knew to be his real name. Then, out loud for everyone's benefit, I proceeded to read the news article itself which followed beneath the pictures.

Well, it was quite a long article but I'll do my best to summarise it for you, along with the rest of the story which subsequently came to light:

About eight years ago, a city stockbroker called Vincent Enfield acquired a yard in Finchley, formerly used for parking vans, from the receiver of a bankrupt delivery business. The reason for the purchase was that he needed somewhere to house his precious collection of classic cars.

In a corner of the yard, above what used to be the offices of the business, there was a small caretaker's flat, and Mr. Enfield employed Roger Duffy as a live-in caretaker – Duffy had, in fact, previously been employed in that capacity by the delivery firm. His duties to Mr. Enfield included not only ensuring the security of the site but also washing and cleaning the cars inside and out and liaising from time to time with the local garage over Enfield's requirements for the servicing and maintenance of each vehicle. He, of course, had a set of keys for every car, needed to perform these duties.

Duffy came in fact from a respectable enough middle-class family. They were originally of Irish descent. No hint, I might add, of a Huguenot connection. On his father's death, Duffy had taken over the family travel agency business. However, the business soon went bust leaving a mountain of debt and many aggrieved holiday-makers faced with losing their holiday bookings. Duffy had simply taken too much money out in salary and bonuses for the good of the business. There were allegations, too, of fraud and tax evasion. Disgraced and unemployed, Duffy was lucky to land the job as a caretaker.

He appeared, however, to be a model employee, reliable, hard-working and honest but, entirely unbeknown to Mr. Enfield, Duffy was carrying on a lucrative business on the side hiring out the cars for weddings and other events, employing friends and cronies as chauffeurs as and when required. He had set up a website to market the business under the title Regency Hire, advertising itself as *Classic cars for classy people.*

If poor Enfield turned up at the yard wanting to take one of his vehicles for a spin and it was not there because it had been hired it out, Duffy would simply inform him that it was at the garage for a minor repair because he'd noticed a loose exhaust, a small dent in the rear bumper, a broken wing mirror or the like. Later, he would present Enfield with a fake invoice which he would say that he had settled himself, whereupon Enfield, praising Duffy for his diligence, would trustingly re-imburse him – effectively a nice little extra bonus.

As if this was not enough, he also used many of these splendid vehicles for his own pleasure, masquerading, as we know, as a posh fellow of substantial means under the assumed name of Duffoy.

As Duffoy, he took to frequenting cafés, bars and restaurants in the Chelsea and South Kensington areas where he would inveigle himself into conversation with other customers, especially regular patrons – just as he did with us – using the opportunity to parade his pretended wealth, status and connections.

I very much doubt either that he'd ever met any of the notable figures or famous celebrities whose names he dropped so copiously. And as for the Hampstead mansion and the luxurious foreign properties he claimed to own, it's obvious that he must have simply downloaded to his mobile phone images from various websites.

Most importantly, of course, on these outings to Chelsea and South Ken, he would drive himself there in whichever of Vincent Enfield's enviable collection of classic cars took his fancy, and always made sure to park it somewhere so that those he sought to impress would get a good look at him arriving or leaving in it. I don't suppose for one moment he had an aged aunt living near our wine bar, as he alleged.

It was mere chance that Duffy's infamous conduct came to light. Another classic car enthusiast was passing a registry office one day and witnessed a couple, just married, coming out of the office and clambering into a car decked out with ribbons. He recognised the car at once as one belonging to his old friend and fellow enthusiast Vincent Enfield. It was a vintage Daimler limousine dating from the late 1960s. He was most surprised that his friend had apparently taken to hiring out one of his precious cars for such an event, unless of course he knew the family. A few days later, he mentioned the matter to Mr. Enfield who was absolutely shocked; he had absolutely no connection with any recently wedded couple or their families and he would never dream of hiring his cars out on a commercial basis. He telephoned Duffy at once who strenuously denied any knowledge of the event.

Enfield remained suspicious, however, and instituted enquiries which eventually led to the whole story coming out. As soon as he knew the facts, he made haste to the yard in Finchley to have it out with Duffy, but the wretched man was nowhere to be found.

As plain Roger Duffy, Duffy was quite happy to cheat and deceive his employer but, as posh Roger Duffoy, he clearly wished to project the image of a perfect gentleman – well-mannered and generous to a fault. Did he just enjoying putting on an act, was he motivated by envy of the well-to-do, or was he simply a fantasist, a Walter Mitty-type character?

He was certainly taking some risk in behaving in the way he did, that someone would eventually suspect something. Had he, perhaps, become so immersed in the character he'd created for himself that he half-believed that he actually owned the priceless cars, the millionaire's mansion in Hampstead, the ritzy foreign properties and all the rest?

Others, like us, would no doubt have been duped by him to believe that he was the smart, wealthy fellow that he pretended to be. He certainly had the ability to charm. But was he a charming dreamer or a charming rogue or a bit of both?

∗∗∗

When Derek had finished his account of this amazing affair, we gaped at each other in astonishment.

"Good Heavens. Quite incredible!" Tom said, reflecting the feelings of us all. "But, tell me, did anyone – Mr Enfield, the press, the Police – ever catch up with Duffy?"

"No, I'm afraid not," Derek responded. "Duffy disappeared without trace. According to the newspaper report, he was last seen by a neighbour driving away from the yard at some speed at the wheel of Mr. Enfield's lovely old Bugatti Roadster."

NINE

A Life in the Country

"Can I introduce an old university friend of mine, Gerald Wrigley?" Tom said, as he arrived at the bar with a pleasant-looking fellow in tow.

"Welcome to our little bar," I said, shaking Gerald's hand, Desmond and the Colonel following suit.

"Gerald and his wife are down here staying with us for a few days. They bought a house in the Cotswolds some years ago not far from the town where I once had my junk shop – though of course I'd sold up by this time to come and live here."

"Junk shop, my foot. I've known Tom for many years and often visited his shop, I can tell you it was a magnificent emporium, full of the most valuable antiques!" Gerald riposted.

"So, do you still live in the Cotswolds, Gerald?" I asked.

"Yes, still in the Cotswolds, but a different house."

"The most beautiful old Elizabethan manor house, I might add," said Tom. "Gerald lives in great style. We are very privileged that he has condescended to grace us with his presence."

"What nonsense!" Gerald replied, laughing. "Don't take any notice of Tom. He's always teasing me. It wasn't always like this. In fact, life looked pretty bleak at one point not so long ago but my wife and I just got very lucky."

"Gerald's story is an interesting one with a nice twist to it." Tom said, injecting a note of intrigue. "You might like to hear it."

"Oh, no, no!" Gerald exclaimed.

"Oh, come on now, please." Desmond pleaded.

"Yes," I said. "We would really like to hear all about it."

"Well, all right. Difficult, though, to know where to start."

"Try the beginning," the Colonel boomed sarcastically. "Usually not a bad place to start."

Well, we both used to work in the City, myself as a banker and Susan, my wife, as an accountant with one of the big firms. We had a lovely flat in Chiswick. We were both doing well but as you might imagine life at work was highly pressurised and often very stressful. Frequently, indeed, we didn't get home till late and there was one period, lasting over a month, when we hardly saw one another.

Susan said to me one day, "What's the point of all this? Why don't we give it all up and go and live in the country?"

She didn't really mean it at the time, but it had implanted a thought in both our minds and in the end that's what we decided to do. We knew of other people who had made much the same decision. Why not us?

We both had some savings and we knew that our London flat would fetch a very good price, leaving a substantial amount over even after paying off the mortgage.

It all took some time of course, but eventually we found our rural idyll, a lovely old Cotswold stone farmhouse with a number of outbuildings which we planned to convert for holiday lets to provide us with some extra income.

To cut a long story short, we eventually obtained planning permission for the conversion of the outbuildings and work began not long afterwards. The farmhouse itself, our new home, was also much in need of renovation. It was all rather more expensive than we had originally bargained for and we had months before us of upheaval, dirt and noise, but we told ourselves it would all be worth it in the end.

The garden and grounds also needed to be sorted. To the front of the house there was a driveway leading to the public road and to the side of the driveway, a wide lawn leading onto a large paddock where one day my wife hoped to keep a few ponies. The driveway was badly potholed, the lawn was in a poor state with moss and many bare patches and the paddock had become a jungle. To the rear of the house was a big kitchen garden which also needed a great deal of attention to bring it back into proper use.

Finally, we finished with the works on the outbuildings and the farmhouse, along with the restoration of the lawn, grounds and kitchen garden, and we were beginning to get used to our new life. It was all so very different from our life in London. The road where we lived in Chiswick was pleasant enough, but here in the country we enjoyed a lovely view over open fields belonging to our neighbour Mr. Rudge, a farmer. There was a farmyard and milking shed, also part of Rudge's farm, which immediately adjoined our kitchen garden. The farmyard was well-kept and the milking shed was not one of those ugly modern milking parlours with concrete walls and a nasty tin roof but a rather handsome old brick-built building. In fact, I quite enjoyed seeing the cows being brought in for milking each day from the adjoining field, along with the daily rural rituals of owls hooting in the evening and cocks crowing in the morning.

It was only a month or so later when we received an unexpected visit from Mr. Rudge. He told us that he had received an offer from a big haulage firm to rent his farmyard as a transport yard which he had reluctantly decided to accept. The fact was, he said, he needed the money and could not pass up such an opportunity.

As you might imagine this was a terrible shock. The quiet country road passing our property would no doubt resonate to the thunderous trundle of lorries and vans day and night – our rural idyll would be shattered and our proposed holiday letting business would hardly be viable. Who would want to put up with the volume and noise of all this traffic?

My wife was on the verge of tears and I was about to vent my disappointment when Mr. Rudge spoke up.

He understood how we must feel about this, he said, and was "prepared to make us an offer for our property."

He said that he thought he could re-locate the milking parlour on part of what was then our garden and one of his sons could occupy the house. He couldn't possibly afford, though, to offer us anything like the price we'd paid, let alone any extra for the cost of all the works we'd carried out, but sadly, in his opinion, we'd have some difficulty in finding another buyer.

My initial reaction was that we had little alternative but to accept Rudge's offer. We would suffer an enormous loss and it would be the end of our dreams of a good life. Our only option would be to return to London.

As it so happened, we had been invited the following evening to dinner with friends of my wife who lived nearby. As we sat down for the first course – smoked trout, I recall – I wasted no time in regaling the assembled company with our tale of woe.

One of the other guests, a very posh surveyor, immediately chimed up, urging us not on any account to accept Rudge's offer.

This surveyor bloke plainly knew what was going on. He happened to know that the haulage company had been looking for some while for a suitable yard for their business. They might have approached Rudge amongst others but, if so, nothing had come of it – because they had recently negotiated the tenancy of another site belonging to one of his – the surveyor's – own clients. What Rudge had told us was a blatant lie.

The truth was that a large development company was looking to acquire sites in the neighbourhood for residential development and the local planning authority was under pressure to allow more housing in the area to serve nearby towns in line with the Local Plan. Rudge's farmyard, milking shed and adjoining field would be an ideal site for such development, being relatively flat and enjoying good road access. However, it would be a much better proposition if our property could be included in the deal. If Rudge could trick us into selling our property to him on the cheap, he could offer it to the developer along with his own property and would stand to gain a substantial additional profit.

"Sit tight" was the surveyor's advice to us. A month or two later we heard that Rudge had negotiated a sale to the developer of his piece of property and, sure enough, shortly after the developer duly approached us with an offer to purchase ours. The sale price, upon which we eventually agreed, was quite staggering – beyond our wildest expectations.

The deal went through remarkably smoothly and as a result we were able to acquire the lovely old manor house which is now our home.

The English countryside has a charm all of its own. We love life in the country and have never regretted leaving London, but our rural dream might so easily have become a rustic nightmare! As we soon learnt, country folk can be every bit as wily as any city slicker.

"And the same is true of old-fashioned seaside towns like Bufferton," Tom remarked. And who among us could possibly disagree?

TEN

More Rumours

I was just coming out of the bank on the corner of Dartmouth Road and Harbour Street when Desmond came rushing up. He seemed rather agitated.

"Glad I've caught up with you, George. There's been a new development in the Colonel and Emily saga, I'm afraid."

"Oh, dear!" I said. "What's it this time?"

"Look, better not talk about it here. I'm meeting Tom at the Harbour Café in ten minutes. Why don't you come along?"

A short walk down Harbour Street took us to the café which is opposite the harbour slipway. There is a wide paved area outside where in the summer months they put out tables and chairs.

Tom was already there, having secured a table at the far end where it was unlikely we would be overheard.

"What's all this about, then?" I said.

"Well," said Desmond, "I was on my way to the post office and I took a short cut down Fishermen's Row, and who should I see come out of one of the little cottages there but the Colonel."

"So?" I said.

"Emily lives in one of the cottages. It belongs, apparently, to friends of her mother, who use it as a holiday home, but they're away for four months visiting family in Australia and have let Emily have it for free until their return. It's one of the reasons she chose specifically to come to work in Bufferton, prior to taking up her teaching appointment."

"Are you sure it was Emily's cottage you saw the Colonel leaving?"

"No, I don't know which is actually hers, but there are only five cottages and, so far as I know, they are all second homes now. I can't imagine why the Colonel might want to visit any of the others."

"Look," I said, "all this is a bit vague, isn't it? You are not absolutely sure that the Colonel was leaving Emily's cottage and even if he was, the evidence is at best circumstantial. There's still no real proof that anything untoward is going on. We've had this sort of conversation before."

"George," said Tom, "you're being too legalistic."

"Well, I was a lawyer, you know."

"Yes, but George," Tom countered, "the world is not a court of law and the truth is the truth – whether or not it can be proved beyond all reasonable doubt or whatever it is you lawyers say. Sometimes one has to rely on feeling and intelligent guesswork in matters like this. There are just too many coincidences here for my liking. And the Colonel has a roving eye … "

"That proves nothing, so do lots of chaps. Roving eyes don't lead automatically to wandering hands, let alone anything worse." I said.

"Yes, yes, all right, all right, I concede – but I still have my suspicions about the Colonel."

"In any case, is it really any of our business what the Colonel gets up to?" I said.

"Damn it all, George, we're his friends. Would we be happy for the Colonel to end up like the bloke with the Russian bride – or your brother for that matter? Surely, we've got a duty at least to say what we think?"

"Oh, I suppose so, but, unless the Colonel says something himself about all this, we still can't say anything to him – or to either of them for that matter – can we? We can hardly urge him not to lose his head over a young girl or accuse her of being a gold-

digger without concrete proof. Think of all the terrible embarrassment if your *feeling* turns out, as I strongly expect, to be wrong."

Neither Tom nor Desmond was able to come up with any immediate answer to this and I remained unconvinced that there was any substance to the rumour. Nevertheless, without me admitting it, they had between them managed to implant a tiny niggle of doubt in my old lawyer's mind.

ELEVEN

Old Friends

Please, reader, forgive me if I have already mentioned it but our little bar is mercifully not one of those noisy establishments, full of the sort of chaps who feel they have to shout at each other, or gatherings of screechy girls on a Friday night out after work.

That's not to say that we're like a public library or a dentists' waiting room where everyone feels they have to be on their best behaviour and whisper if they need to communicate. There's just a relaxing aura about the Back Bar and a gentle hubbub of happy voices. Nobody feels a need to raise their voice, except, of course for the Colonel's occasional booming contributions to the conversation.

There was a bloke, however, who took matters to the opposite extreme. He'd visited the bar on several successive nights, always alone. He never spoke to anyone except to order a drink and sat very quietly in a corner by himself. Now, we like to feel that we regulars are a friendly lot and that we do our best to welcome newcomers without being too pushy – especially if they are on their own – but this fellow didn't seem at all interested. One couldn't accuse him of being stand-offish exactly, because he always smiled pleasantly and nodded politely, but that was it.

In fact it took the Colonel in true booming form to bring the chap out of his shell. He was addressing the three of us but his voice could be heard from one end of the bar to the other ...

"Do you know what?" He boomed.

"What?" We duly chorused.

"Well, I was at a funeral at the church over at Nettlecombe

yesterday, of an old army friend, Bill Perry, and the service was conducted by a tall clergyman about the same age as me – and there was just something about him that seemed familiar. I cast my mind back to other occasions – weddings, baptisms, funerals – which I might have attended at the same church or elsewhere in this area, but drew a blank. At the wake afterwards, however, held here at the Bufferton Sands Hotel, this tall clerical fellow came up to speak to me.

"Hello, Gordon," he said, "you don't remember me, do you?"

I had to admit that I didn't.

"I'm Toby Mitcham."

The years rolled away and it all came back to me. Toby, Bill and I had been at Sandhurst together. Toby was always a mischievous lad, a bit of a tearaway, smoked like a factory chimney, drank like a shoal of fishes, always chasing after the girls, the last person I would have expected to become a clergyman. It transpired that he had spent ten years in the army before leaving to take holy orders.

"By God, Toby," I said. "So you are!"

The Colonel was about to elaborate further when he was interrupted by the quiet bloke who came to join us at the bar. He had obviously been listening in to the Colonel's booming oration.

"I hope you won't think me rude for butting in, but I have a little story too which perhaps you gentleman might like to hear?"

"Yes, of course," I said, the others hastening to agree.

"I'm Donald Holman incidentally. I work in London as an actuary with an insurance company. I'm down here for ten days, staying with my mother, who's just moved into one of those converted coastguard cottages at Bufferton Cove."

We all introduced ourselves to him and having bought the fellow a drink, he launched into his story:

Most evenings, on my way home from work, I like to go for a drink at a local pub not far from where I live. It's never too busy, at least early in the evening, and I'm quite happy to enjoy a quiet drink on my own, but one Friday evening I got into conversation with a chap called Peter Rickworth, with whom I struck up an unlikely friendship, unlikely given that we were so very different in many respects.

Peter was a social worker employed by the local borough council, and obviously the nature of our working lives could not have been more dissimilar. Without wishing to imply that all social workers share the same views, Peter's opinions were invariably of a leftish kind and I am generally of a different persuasion. Indeed we were, it would be fair to say, on opposite sides of the political and almost every other fence. Peter was an extroverted, outgoing sort of chap, while I tend to be more reserved.

To work I wear a sober grey suit with standard black leather shoes and I try to keep my hair well-trimmed and tidy. Peter, on the other hand, wore a leather jacket, denims and trainers and sported a pony tail and a rather ridiculous long straggly beard.

Despite our obvious differences, I found Peter to be a thoroughly likeable sort of fellow with a lively sense of humour. Though we invariably disagreed about almost everything, our conversations never became acrimonious and we always managed to have a good laugh. I enjoyed his company and like to think that he enjoyed mine.

Peter used to come regularly to the pub every Friday evening, but one Friday he failed to appear as usual. At the time I thought nothing of it, but he failed to appear on the following Friday and the next one too. Weeks became months and months became years, over four years in fact, during which time he never re-appeared and I had all but forgotten him.

Then, one Friday evening, as I was standing at the bar, waiting to be served, a man sidled up beside me.

"Hello, Donald", he said.

I simply had no idea who he was.

"You obviously don't remember me," he said. "I'm Peter Rickworth."

I peered at him again, and this time I just about recognised his face, but he'd changed so very much. Gone were the pony tail and straggly beard. He was clean-shaven now, with well-groomed hair. Gone, too, were the leather jacket and denims, replaced by a well-tailored, navy blue pin-stripe suit complete with a double-breasted waistcoat and gold watch chain, and in place of the trainers, a shiny pair of smart black brogues.

I said how delighted I was to see him again after such a long time, and asked, innocently, how things were in the world of social work.

"Oh," he replied, "I don't do that any more. I work in the City for a firm of investment managers ... as a wealth management consultant."

TWELVE

A Shriek in the Night

We had only just arrived at the bar and were yet to order our first round of drinks when we were joined by Jean Amesbury. Jean sadly lost her husband Andrew to a heart attack some years ago, and had taken to coming to the pub most Saturday evenings before repairing to the Bridge Club.

Jean is a bubbly, larger-than-life type of person, a sort of older if rather less earthy version of our former barmaid Gloria. Perhaps inevitably, she is universally known as the Merry Widow. We always invite her to join us at the bar.

"Haven't seen you for a little while, Jean," the Colonel said. "You weren't in last Saturday?"

"No, I was away for a few days up in Shropshire. It was a most enjoyable visit – but something really rather weird happened while I was there."

"We're all ears. Do tell us all about it." I said. "But, before you start, let's get you a drink. What'll it be, your usual?"

"Oh, yes please, gin and tonic, but if I've got to entertain you lot with my story, I think I deserve a double!"

"Coming right up."

After Jean had settled herself comfortably on her stool and taken a sip of her gin and tonic, she cleared her throat and began to tell her remarkable story:

WELL, SIR MARK WAINSCOTT, a cousin of my dear husband on his mother's side of the family, recently inherited on the death of his father a beautiful manor house in the countryside not far from

Ludlow, called Tastlewick Hall, which has been in the Wainscott family for centuries. It is a black and white Tudor building, quite large, all higgledy-piggledy … you know the sort of thing. But of course houses like that take a fair bit of maintenance – they're not cheap to keep up – so Mark decided to turn part of it into an up-market B&B while he and Lady Sarah, his charming wife, would continue to occupy the remaining part, comprising all of the east wing.

On Wednesday last week I was at home doing the ironing, while watching daytime TV. All the adverts seemed to be for insurance plans to cover funeral expenses, stairlifts or special bath units designed for the elderly and infirm – most depressing! I was half way through with the job when the phone rang. It was Mark.

He had had a late cancellation, so he told me, and wondered if I might like to come and stay for the weekend, Friday to Monday, as his guest at Tastlewick Hall – *a non-paying* guest, naturally. It was most generous of him. Well of course, I jumped at the opportunity. I had been there several times before with my husband when Mark's father was still alive and before the establishment of the B&B. It's a quite magical place and I couldn't wait to go there again.

And it didn't disappoint. It was just as lovely as I remembered it – full of amazing antiques, tapestries and paintings.

Mark showed me to my room, the best in the house so he said. There was a four-poster bed, a lovely old medieval chest, a Regency *chaise longue*, and a splendid wardrobe in the Art Nouveau style. The view from the widow over the gardens and countryside beyond was sublime.

Along with a large tapestry of hunting scenes, there were also some beautiful pictures in the room. One in particular stood out. It depicted Lady Arabella Wainscott, who was married to the sixth or seventh Baronet – I forget which – and lived at the manor in the early nineteenth century, the Regency Period. She was a beautiful young woman, though of a feisty disposition. Her face in the portrait bore a determined expression and she looked as if she was about to give someone a piece of her mind. It was a wonderful painting and the artist had managed to capture the *essence* of her character, not simply her appearance. She could have walked straight out of the pages of a novel by Jane Austen, and one felt that if one looked for long enough at the painting she would actually open her mouth to speak.

Lady Arabella was something of a legend in the family and I recall Mark's father us telling the story, with evident relish, over dinner during one of our visits, leaving no salacious detail to the imagination and, no doubt, adding a few embellishments of his own. Put shortly, Arabella had returned one evening from visiting her sister in Hereford to find her husband cavorting about with two naked kitchen-maids in the matrimonial bedchamber. Her angry shriek was heard all over the house. She flounced off that very evening, leaving her husband and their two children, never to return.

Rumours abounded as to Arabella's life thereafter: one that she lived with the owner of a sugar plantation in Jamaica but on finding him one day taking his pleasure with a slave girl, had made off with a pirate captain with whom she sailed the seven seas for evermore; another that she became the mistress of a Venetian nobleman at a *palazzo* on the Grand Canal in Venice. A further, more prosaic but perhaps more plausible account has her down as spending the rest of her life as a schoolmistress at a small village school somewhere in Yorkshire.

The bedchamber in which her husband was discovered playing naughty games with kitchen-maids was, in fact, the very bedroom in which I was to spend my stay.

At weekends, dinner for B&B guests was also provided – a quite grand affair held in the Great Hall. Dinner on the Saturday evening of my stay was, however, disturbed by two of the other guests, whom I assumed to be husband and wife, having a row conducted *sotto voce* at first but becoming louder. I happened to be seated at the next table and while I was unable to catch every word, I got the gist of it: the wife had come home one day that week earlier than expected from visiting her mother, to find her husband in bed with the Portuguese *au pair*. The girl was instantly dismissed but the wife had just discovered that her husband had texted the girl on several occasions since ... and they'd apparently been seen together by a friend in a bar. The volume continued to rise and the wife's tone became increasingly strident until finally she rose from the table, stamping her feet and shrieking at her husband with a stream of choice expletives. The couple thereupon left the Great Hall, the husband mumbling apologies to the other guests as he passed. There was much raising of eyebrows and pursing of lips but of course being British nobody said anything.

After dinner, Mark, who liked to play the *maître d'* on these occasions, approached me to say that he was sorry about the disturbance and hoped that it had not spoilt my dinner.

On the contrary, I said that I had rather enjoyed the drama and remarked that the row had reminded me of the story of Lady Arabella, the circumstances of which were somewhat similar. In fact, the woman concerned even seemed to me to bear a striking resemblance to Arabella in her portrait in the bedroom. Mark agreed and we both had a good laugh although Mark added, with a smile, that he rather doubted the woman at dinner was destined to become the mistress of a Venetian nobleman at a *palazzo* on the Grand Canal.

After my chat with Mark, I retired to bed and fell into a deep sleep, but was woken in the early hours by the sound of a loud shrieking voice. Oh, my God! That woman is having another go at her husband, I thought.

I mentioned the incident to Mark the next morning, but he said that was simply impossible. After leaving the Great Hall, the woman had slapped her husband in the face, flounced off into the darkness, much as Lady Arabella had done, and had driven off in their car not to return – leaving her husband to spend the night alone.

I wondered whether the shriek in the night had been simply my imagination or a bad dream, or was it perhaps Arabella's howl of rage echoing down the centuries?

THIRTEEN

Invisibility

It was one of those days when nothing much had happened. There was nothing much of interest on the national news to provoke argument or discussion and no new scandal in the town for us to gossip about. We had, frankly, quite run out of conversation. Even, Desmond, never one normally short of words, was uncharacteristically quiet. However, the evening was unexpectedly redeemed by a stranger, who came in and treated us to another story about changing identity – this was of a rather different nature to the one about a social worker turned City gent.

"Good walk?" The Colonel asked the stranger as he stepped up to the bar to order his drink. He was certainly attired for a walk – a stout pair of walking boots with his trousers tucked into a pair of long, thick woollen socks.

"Well, not exactly," he replied. "You see, my wife is very keen that I should take more exercise. We are staying at the Bufferton Sands Hotel which now, as I'm sure you know, has a gym, or *fitness centre* as they call it, in the basement. She proposed that we do an hour's worth of training on the ghastly exercise machines there. I said immediately that I'd prefer to go for a cliff walk. I meant it at the time but, when I got to the bottom of the path, it looked so terribly steep that I'm afraid to say I thought better of the whole enterprise. So, what was I to do? Well, I remembered passing this pub on the way, so of course I retraced my steps and here I am!"

"Sensible fellow!" Said Desmond. "But wait a minute – I think we've met before. Weren't you in the cocktail bar at the Bufferton Sands before lunch yesterday?"

"Yes, I was as a matter of fact."

"I thought so. You were sitting next to my old friend and colleague from work, Jeff Peters, with whom I was due to have lunch. I hadn't seen him for years and frankly I didn't recognise him at first. He was much fatter, redder in the face and had grown a great, bristly moustache."

"Funny you should say that," the man said, "but I had a similar experience with an old friend of mine the other day – but, in the case of your friend, it was simply a matter of nature's *changing course untrimmed* – as the Bard put it, whereas with my friend, it was a matter of deception and duplicity!"

"Oh, we're always keen to hear stories about deception and duplicity", I said. "Do tell us about it, please."

"Well, if you insist ... "

"We do!"

WELL, IT ALL BEGAN, you see, on a Sunday. Sundays are always the same. I start with a firm resolve to undertake some form of healthy outdoor exercise to make up for a week spent all day sitting at my office desk, battling against the ceaseless flow of emails eroding my patience and silting up my brain. Rarely, however, do I seem to achieve my objective. The Sunday of my unexpected meeting with Max was no exception.

I had decided on this occasion that, weather permitting, I would take a walk in the countryside. Indeed, I had purchased yet another book of walks to add to my existing collection of walking guides featuring enticing woodland trails, coastal paths and country strolls, of which only two of the shorter ones, I regret to admit, have I ever succeeded in actually walking.

I had chosen a circular walk from my new book which started and finished in a village only about an hour's drive away from home. The walk took in, so the book promised, the ruins of a

Norman castle, two pretty village churches and a stretch of water meadow noted for its rare butterflies. It was not too long, just three miles, nor were there any worrying warnings about muddy paths, slippery slopes or steep inclines to put me off. This time I was quite determined to do the thing.

I am, frankly, a bit of a late starter on Sunday mornings and decided that I would do my walk in the afternoon. This was a mistake.

The trouble was that, after lunch, my enthusiasm for walking or doing anything else very much had largely deserted me. Sunday lunch had induced in me that feeling of lazy torpor so characteristic of Sunday afternoons. As P. G. Wodehouse might have put it, I was not exactly inert, but I was very far from being ert. I yawned.

"Well?" said my wife, Margaret.

"Well, what?" I replied, rather testily.

"I thought you said you were going for a walk?"

Margaret had been nagging me for months about my expanding waistline and the need to do something about it. Unless I promised to take more exercise, I was threatened with the gym and even, for God's sake, a personal trainer.

"Yes", I said, "I'm just off, dear."

I made a great play of putting on my Barbour and fetching my walking boots, though I had no intention of *actually* doing the walk, of course. I had quite another plan. I would drive the short distance down to my office in the High Street and take a little nap there, after which I would simply skip across the road to the Willow Café for a nice pot of tea and a Danish pastry. Thereafter, it would only be a matter of making a brief detour to the local park to muddy the boots before returning home. Job done!

My office comprises two floors of an attractive red brick mid-Georgian building above an antique shop in the upper part of the High Street. This is the old historic quarter of town and the street here is cobbled and closed to motor traffic. Nearby are the well-preserved old covered market and Victorian Town Hall. The Willow is diagonally opposite my office and occupies the ground floor of a half-timbered medieval building of great architectural interest. As the tourist hand-out proudly proclaims in customary brochure-speak, *The upper part of the High Street oozes history, character and charm.* In contrast, the lower part of the street, with its soulless modern shop fronts, miserably fails to ooze any of these characteristics, except perhaps for the old Art-Deco cinema. However, even that's now been converted into a pizzeria, bar and disco, necessitating a 10-mile drive to the nearest multiplex to see a film, making old grumpies like me even grumpier.

I felt rather pleased with myself that afternoon – the first part of my plan had worked a treat and I emerged from my nap in the office blinking in the afternoon sunshine and much refreshed.

At the bottom end of the High Street, completely spoiling the view of the canal, stands a new warehouse-like building, euphemistically called the Waterside Leisure Centre. This horrid structure accommodates all the usual facilities, including an aerobic studio, sauna and plunge pool and, of course, the dreaded gymnasium where lurk the sinister instruments of torture otherwise known as exercise machines – and awaiting me if Margaret should ever discover that I had deceived her.

Trying to blot out this awful prospect I crossed the road to the Willow Café and plumped myself down with relief at my usual table by the fireplace. I hadn't been there long when a man suddenly loomed up and asked if I'd mind if he joined me. Well, I did mind, of course, but what could one say?

"Please do," I said.

He was a large fellow with a mop of untidy curly hair and a big, bushy beard. He wore an old sports jacket patched at the elbows over an open-necked check shirt, corduroy trousers and heavy brown brogues. He peered at me intently in a manner which I found quite disconcerting.

"Hello, Paul", he said.

I was totally perplexed. How did he know my name? I was sure I'd never seen him before.

I simply didn't know who he was, which I admitted.

Chuckling, he responded that I certainly ought to know as, apparently, we used to play snooker together every Wednesday evening. "It's your old friend Max," he said, though, rather oddly, he confessed that he now went by another name.

Good Lord! I thought. *Max.* How extraordinary! He looked quite different and though I would never have recognised him if he hadn't told me, I could see it now.

When I first knew Max he was a successful businessman with a finger in a number of very profitable local pies. He lived in a substantial Victorian villa just outside the town with a huge garden and swimming pool. He always drove a big swanky car of some sort and with his well-groomed hair slightly greying at the temples and smartly tailored suits, cut an image of affluent respectability. Witty, urbane and charming, he was the ideal dinner party guest and a highly esteemed member of local society.

However, about two years ago rumours began to circulate of serious fraud and misconduct in his business dealings. Both the police and revenue authorities were investigating. Nor did the scandal end there. It transpired that Max had enjoyed a string of affairs with married women whose unwitting husbands were prominent members of the local business and professional fraternity. The press of course had a field day and the town hung its head in collective shame that such goings-on had been allowed to happen under our very noses. But of Max, the fraudster and serial seducer, there was nothing to be seen. He had disappeared without trace.

Astounded, I asked him where he'd been and why he'd come back.

"I never actually went away," he said.

The newspapers at the time, he reminded me, had reported that he had vanished into thin air – that he had become invisible. To be invisible means, of course, unable to be seen, but he pointed out that the concepts of visibility and invisibility are flexible ones, that men of vision claim to *see the future*, that Milton, describing Hell in *Paradise Lost*, writes of *darkness visible* while in the City of London they talk about *invisible earnings*. What a joke! And, of course, he rightly maintained that one may *see* in the primary sense of observing but without really seeing the true picture – adding that he remained flesh and blood not – "some gaseous substance diffused in the ether." That when someone looked at him they saw "a man in the street" but not who he *actually* was. "One doesn't, he insisted, have to do a bunk to the Antipodes or some resort on the Spanish Costas in order to disappear. All you have to do," he argued, "is to make yourself invisible to those who might know you."

"Do you mean all those people you cheated and whose lives you ruined?" I exclaimed furiously, threatening to expose him.

"Do I not detect," he instantly responded, "a blast of moral flatulence, the crude belch of righteous indignation?" He accused me of being an old hypocrite because, he claimed, I had myself been "guilty of a little extra-marital dalliance with a busty, young bimbo" less than half my age.

This was nonsense. One evening, before Max's disappearance, I had gallantly escorted a young lady home after an office party as her flat was on the way to my house. She had had rather too much to drink and when we got to the entrance porch at the block of flats where she lived she suddenly thrust herself at me, kissing and throwing her arms around me in a most unseemly manner. I extricated myself as soon as I could but not before Max, who happened to be passing in his car, had seen her clinging to me like a wet towel. He had obviously assumed the worst as his sort always do. In fact, I'd told Margaret all about it and she'd laughed herself silly, but Max clearly thought he had some hold over me which would be enough to buy my silence.

It was outrageous! I was about to spring to my feet and denounce the scoundrel when who should enter the café but Margaret and a friend of hers from the Tennis Club. God! What if she saw me – I was supposed to be out taking a healthy walk not lounging about in a tea shop! Ghastly visions of treadmills and things at the leisure centre welled up in my mind.

Max asked what was the matter – I must have gone quite pale.

I told him that Margaret had just come in and I briefly explained the situation.

"I knew you had something to hide," he said – insisting that I made straight for the gents' toilet before she saw me, urging me to walk slowly and without looking back.

Like a robot I did what he said. Soon he joined me there.

He got me to change coats with him, my Barbour for his sports jacket. Next, he took from his pocket one of those floppy fishing hats. He told me to put it on and pull it well down, follow him back to the table and sit in the chair facing the fireplace.

I did as I was told.

Katie, one of the regular waitresses, came to take our order.

Max boldly ordered us both the Champagne tea – which is the same as the Full English Tea on the menu but with the addition of smoked salmon sandwiches and a glass of Champagne. He asked Katie to bring the Champagne right away.

I was too dazed to object. Perhaps this whole mad episode was just a bad dream, I thought. Soon I would awake in a bright meadow alive with the fluttering of rare butterflies, book of walks in hand – if only!

Nervously I looked over my shoulder. Margaret was happily chatting away to her friend. She may have seen a man in a funny hat, but she obviously hadn't seen me. To all intents and purposes, I was invisible to her.

The Champagne arrived, and the weirdest of things happened. It was if someone had flicked a switch in my brain. I tried to resist but was quite unable to control the facial muscles, and my face creased in a broad grin. A mood of boyish exuberance overcame me. This was fun!

Max chuckled.

Katie tittered.

I giggled.

"I give you a toast, Paul," said Max raising his glass:

"To invisibility!"

It seemed churlish, in the circumstances, not to respond and I raised my own glass to his with a little clink.

"To Invisibility! Glorious Invisibility!" I gladly replied.

FOURTEEN

Tuscan Escapade

It was a few minutes after six on a warm summer evening when an attractive lady entered the bar with a Jack Russell terrier.

"Is it all right to bring the dog in here?" she inquired.

"Of course, dogs are not allowed in the Terrace Bar but they are permitted in this one provided they are well-behaved and kept on a lead," the Colonel assured her. He had always had a soft spot for dogs not to mention, if Tom and Desmond were right, attractive ladies.

"Oh, good," she said with evident relief.

"What's his name?" Desmond asked.

"Lucky."

Wuff, wuff. Lucky barked, looking up at us with his beady eyes and furiously wagging his tail.

"So, what brought you to our little bar, if you don't mind me asking?" I said.

"Well, we're staying with our friends, Neil and Suzie, at their holiday cottage near Bufferton Cove. Rupert, that's my husband, and Neil are playing golf and Suzie's been away all day visiting her aunt in Totnes, so I was left alone with Lucky. We had a lovely walk all the way here from the cottage along the cliff path. Rupert said that this was the most civilised pub in Bufferton for a refreshing drink. He said he'd come to pick us up from here at about 7 o'clock. Sorry, I'm Olivia, by the way."

"This is Tom, Desmond and the Colonel – I mean to say Gordon – and I'm George," I said.

"So, to use that awful new expression, you're having a

staycation this year, are you?" Tom asked.

"Oh, No!" Olivia answered. "Actually, the four of us have just returned from Tuscany. It was the most extraordinary holiday ... "

"Really? Do tell us about it," the Colonel said.

"Well, I don't want to bore you. I feel I've intruded enough as it is."

"Oh, you won't bore us – not at all!" I said.

"Well, all right, if you'd really like to hear about it ...

YOU SEE, WE PLANNED to go on holiday with our friends, Neil and Suzie, and they suggested Italy as the perfect destination. We both agreed and I was left to organise something. It's always me, in fact, left to do the organising. I thought Tuscany would be a good choice and I found this simply marvellous place on the internet called *Castello di Boscone*, a well-preserved fifteenth-century castle. It was described as being set in the heart of the Tuscan countryside, north of Castellina in Chianti, surrounded by its own vineyards and olive groves. I must say it was a beautifully produced website with lovely pictures of the castle and the estate ... not to mention spectacular views of rolling hills and forests stretching far into the distance.

The castle was not a hotel but, as the blurb put it, *a guest-house, the ancestral home of the Pontini family* who still own it and live there and that we would be guests of Count Ludovico Pontini and his wife. Well, that is to say *paying guests*. It was very expensive – much more than we would normally expect to spend – but at least the deal included not only bed and breakfast but also an evening meal with wine. It looked like this would be the holiday of a lifetime. Everyone agreed and we reserved two double rooms for a fortnight. I booked flights to Pisa and car hire.

I must say I could hardly wait to get there. I think we all were very excited. Finally, the day came, and we were not disappointed.

As we approached the castle up a long drive lined by cypress trees, it seemed even more magnificent than the photographs.

Our host the Count was the soul of kindness and did everything to make us feel welcome and comfortable. The bedrooms, all with ensuite facilities, were positively luxurious and the meals, taken in the gorgeous dining hall with its marble columns and frescoed ceiling, were delicious. Dinner was served with superb Chianti from the estate's own vineyards and other excellent Italian wines. Our party and the two other couples staying at the castle, also from England, were all equally delighted.

On, I think, the fifth night of our stay the Count and his wife Grazia joined us for dinner. I couldn't believe it but the Count produced several bottles of *Sassicaia* – as you may know one of the most precious of all Italian wines. During the course of this epic meal the Count, who spoke heavily accented but understandable English, asked how we were all enjoying our stay and whether we liked the castle. Did we find it perhaps a little *old-fashioned* for modern tastes? We assured him that this was not the case, that we thought the castle was beautiful, that we loved it to bits and were enjoying our stay.

The Count seemed glad that we approved. He had had no alternative, he said, but to take in paying guests because of the enormous cost of upkeep – though he was at pains to make clear how much he enjoyed our company and what a *pleasure* it was to entertain us. The countess smiled sweetly, and nodded in agreement.

He then invited us to buy some of his *Chianti* or special 'Super-Tuscan' wine. He could arrange delivery to UK for only a small charge and would give us a special *sconto* – a big discount for cash only and *Niente carta di Credito*, no credit cards. After this pronouncement he became even more forthcoming about his financial difficulties. He even asked us to consider making a donation to the chapel restoration fund.

I must say we were all a little taken aback by this outburst and conversation ground to a halt for a few moments, but the effects of the wonderful wine and food soon clicked in again and the happy chatter and laughter resumed. We all agreed that we would invest in a few cases of wine. It would, no doubt, be good value and would help the Count a little with his finances.

A few nights later the Count joined us for drinks before dinner. He was all smiles on this occasion and no pleas of poverty. He recommended that we might consider a visit next day to the monastery of Sant'Antimo near the town of Montalcino, south of Siena. As if to underline his suggestion, thoughtful as always, one of the wines served at dinner was a delicious Brunello di Montalcino, another great Tuscan wine. We agreed on the proposed excursion and Suzie and I retired for an early night so as to be fresh in the morning. Neil and Rupert remained behind for a nightcap.

I was nearly asleep when Rupert came up to bed. He seemed a bit agitated and I asked what the matter was. He had had, he told me, a most extraordinary conversation with Neil while they sipped their Grappa together. Neil, he said, was proposing to make the Count an offer for one of his paintings, a smallish one on the wall near the great fireplace in the dining hall.

I should, perhaps, explain at this point that Neil works for one of the big fine-art auction houses in London and is an acknowledged expert in early Italian art. He was absolutely convinced that this panting was an original work by the early Sienese painter Duccio di Buoninsegna. If he was right it would be fabulously valuable.

Since none of the other paintings in the castle were, in Neil's opinion, of any great value being mainly nineteenth-century copies, he strongly suspected that the Count had no idea that he owned a Duccio. Further, he was strapped for cash.

Neil's idea was to offer £3,000 for the painting. He offered to cut Rupert in on the deal, if Rupert would like to go halves with him. Neil said he could arrange for the funds to be transferred to an account at a local bank so that he could pay the Count quickly and in cash as an added inducement. Rupert could pay his share, if he wished, when we returned to England. If the deal came off, Neil would arrange to leave the painting in the custody of an art dealer friend of his in Rome. Needless to say, if the attribution to Duccio was confirmed, and the painting was eventually sold at auction, it would fetch an absolute fortune. We would be joining the ranks of the mega-rich.

Well, I said that I didn't like the idea at all. It seemed absolutely wrong to try to take advantage of the poor old Count who had been so very good to us. Rupert was in complete agreement and had told Neil that he wanted no part in the matter. We were both frankly very surprised that Neil could even contemplate making such an offer and considered the whole thing most unethical to say the least. Indeed, we were sure that his employers in London would take a very dim view if they were ever to find out. In fact, Rupert felt that we had a moral duty to warn the Count of Neil's intended approach and at least to suggest that he took expert professional advice before giving consideration to any offer. I agreed but we were put in something of a quandary. Neil is Rupert's best friend. They were at school together, and Suzie and I are also very close. Indeed, we see more of them than any of our other friends put together. We regard them almost as family. If Neil ever discovered that we had tipped the Count off and crabbed the deal of a lifetime, it would almost certainly result in the end of our friendship.

Next morning we decided that, come what may, we simply had to say something to Count Pontini. Rupert went down before breakfast to try and find him, but he was busy, so we resolved that we should have a further try before dinner while Neil and Suzie were in their room, showering and changing.

As arranged, we set off directly after breakfast for Sant'Antimo, Neil, Suzie, Rupert and I along with the other two couples staying at the castle, in two cars.

It was a most enjoyable day. The monastery is a magical place lying in a valley amidst the most wonderful scenery. Well worth the visit if you have never been there. Afterwards we spent some time exploring the nearby vineyards where they make the famous Brunello wine which we had enjoyed the previous evening, followed by a visit to the attractive small town of Montalcino itself. It was very hot, though, and Rupert and I were in an anxious mood. We couldn't wait to return and get our meeting with the Count over with.

I was really quite relieved when we finally turned into the familiar driveway leading up to the castle. But as we drew near the castle itself, we were surprised to see a man standing in the middle of the drive, blocking our passage. Rupert, who was driving, stopped and opened the car window, whereupon the man came round to speak to us. He was tall, well-dressed and very distinguished-looking.

"Good evening. May I ask what your business is here?" He said in impeccable English with only the merest hint of an Italian accent. The conversation which ensued is engraved on my memory ...

"Well, we are staying at the castle as guests of Count Pontini," Rupert answered.

"Oh no, you're not." said the tall man.

"What on earth do you mean?"

"I mean that I am Count Ludovico Pontini and you are not my guests. I'm afraid that you are the victims of a fraud as indeed I have been."

We gasped in astonishment.

By this time the other two couples staying at the castle had also arrived, and the situation was briefly explained to them. The men were quite speechless and the women in tears, including me.

The Count proceeded to explain what had occurred, which he had only himself discovered that day when he and his wife had returned from the United States. He was, he told us, an art historian and had been invited to deliver a series of lectures at universities and academic institutions across America on aspects of Renaissance Italian art and culture. He and his wife had been away for the best part of 18 months, and on their arrival home at the castle had found a police inspector waiting to see them.

I'll do my best to summarise what the Count had to say next:

Shortly after he left for America this man, whom we believed to be the Count, and the woman, apparently his wife, took possession of the castle. The Count's former estate manager had retired due to ill health three months earlier and been replaced by a new manager. The man had provided excellent references and the Count was relieved to have found a suitable replacement. The references, however, were fake. This new man was in fact in league with the rogues pretending to be the Count and his wife, and had assisted in facilitating their dastardly plan. They were partners in crime and, according to the police, on the lookout for new scams to inflict on an innocent public.

How they came to learn of the Count's impending trip to America and when he and his wife would be away from the castle, remains a mystery, but the police suspected that they may have been tipped off by someone employed by the agency which had made their travel arrangements.

During the Count's time in America there would, no doubt,

have been many innocent guests, like us, charged handsomely for their stay at the castle.

The Count explained that he occasionally hosted academic courses and seminars on topics of artistic and cultural interest and that he had a brochure prepared to send out to interested parties. Somehow these rogues must have got hold of a copy and used it as a template for a website – altering the wording in such a way as suited their nefarious purposes.

Before leaving for the States, the Count had given all his domestic staff at the castle leave of absence, and they were employed far away at a hotel in the Dolomites. The crooks employed new staff – that is to say a chef and two maids – none of whom were local and would therefore be unaware of the deception.

The estate workers who tended the Castle vineyards and olive groves had little reason ever to visit the castle itself, only the winery where the wine was made, the *cantina* where wine and olives were stored, and the estate office all of which were located in outbuildings.

Nevertheless, these con artists were taking a terrible risk. At any moment, they could have been exposed. Rogues, however, have a way of getting away with things, provided they have the bravado and cheek to carry it off. And indeed they did get away with it for a long while, though they only just avoided capture in the end.

It so happened that the Count's last speaking engagement in America was cancelled and he and his wife had decided to fly home earlier than expected. An email to this effect was sent to the estate office, advising that they expected to arrive in the afternoon of the following day. The crooks – all three of them – made hurried arrangements to leave the following morning and, no doubt, we were encouraged to embark on an outing so that we would not be there to witness their departure.

These awful people were in fact wanted for questioning in connection with previous scams and frauds committed in other parts of Italy, but, so far, they had managed to evade arrest and their whereabouts weren't known. However, the police received a tip-off from an underworld informer leading them to the castle. Unfortunately, they arrived just too late. The birds, as they say, had flown.

"God have mercy on us," I cried out loud, when the Count had finished speaking.

"You do well to invoke the pity of the Almighty," he replied.

Blubbing, I told the Count how sorry we all were. We had no idea. None of us had suspected a thing.

The Count was very sympathetic and regretted that our holiday had been spoilt in this manner. He kindly invited us to remain for the night, but was sorry that he would have to ask us to leave in the morning. In an effort to console us, he emphasised that his misfortunes were much worse than ours. Not only had he suffered the invasion of his home by imposters and the theft of his identity but, when these rogues departed, they took with them many items of value stolen from the castle – including much of the family silver and porcelain dating from the seventeenth and eighteenth centuries, several priceless antique clocks, a pair of rare duelling pistols, his entire collection of Roman pottery, his last two cases of Sassicaia and, most valuable of all, a painting of the Blessed Virgin and Child attributed to the famous painter Duccio di Buoninsegna.

FIFTEEN

A Dog's Life

Wuff, wuff. I'm called Lucky, and not just Lucky by name, mind you, but truly fortunate as well.

I love my master Rupert and his wife Olivia. They are very kind to me and I believe they love me too. You humans talk of 'a dog's life' to mean something bad, but mine is a good life, a happy life, but this was not always the case. I was first owned by a horrid woman called Lana Kendall, the singer and actress.

Lana bought me as a puppy and at more or less the same time acquired a beautiful Burmese kitten with a coat of shiny dark brown fur and very yellow eyes. She called the kitten Jam and she called me Sponge. I suppose she thought this was funny, but these are scarcely suitable names for a proud aristocratic cat and a self-respecting dog. In fact, we were not treated like proper pets at all but as sort of fashion accessories, simply props to support Lana's image – wheeled out for photo shoots but otherwise ignored.

On the surface, Lana was all sugary sentimentality and sweet innocence, the way she wanted to be portrayed in the media, but in reality, she was as hard as nails and twice as sharp. Unlike other celebrities from humble backgrounds, as Lana was, she sought to distance herself from her relations and former friends; she wanted nothing to do with the working-class area in which she was brought up, and never once visited her childhood home on the council estate where her mother still lived. What a contrast with her younger sister, Mary. Mary was just as beautiful as Lana and had become a successful fashion model, but she had felt no desire to divorce herself from her roots and did her best to ensure that some of her success rubbed off for the benefit of the local community from which she and Lana came. I so wished Mary could have been my mistress in place of her older sister.

Three things mattered most to Lana: fame, money and status. She had fame, she had money – though she was not fully satisfied yet with her position on the Rich List – but status was a rather more elusive commodity. Money, she believed, was not enough in itself to confer status, not in England anyway; some other ingredient was required which she identified as *class*. And so she had bought an enormous mansion in the Cotswolds (because that's where a lot of really *classy* people seemed to live) and sought a suitably classy husband to install in it. Thus she would herself acquire *class*, as pale skin acquires a tan when exposed to the sun. That's the way her calculating mind worked.

The only times that Jam and I were truly happy were during Lana's absences in America and elsewhere for filming or shows. During these periods we stayed with Fred, Lana's head gardener and Sadie his wife. They were what you humans call the salt of the earth, the nicest, kindest people you could imagine. Fred took me for lovely long walks and Jam could always count on some fresh fish for supper and a good stroke from Sadie.

We dogs understand more than you humans give us credit for. We look, we listen, we empathise, we absorb, we have memories even longer than elephants. We have senses you humans lack. I can look into my master Rupert's face and read his innermost thoughts, understand his feelings and share his deepest memories.

I wish I could tell the polite old gentlemen at the bar how I came to escape from Lana and to belong to Rupert and also how I was responsible for getting him and Olivia together. I can't speak human but If I could, this is the story I would tell:

Well, to begin right at the beginning, Rupert, who was not then my master, was motoring along a country road in the Cotswolds on his way back to Cheltenham from visiting an elderly client. Life, frankly, had not been very satisfactory since he had left the Army. His first civilian job was with a firm of insurance brokers in the City of London, to which his uncle had kindly introduced him and had, frankly, been a bit of a disappointment. These days, the City teems with horribly earnest young men and women frenetically e-mailing each other from dawn to dusk. The cosy clubability, the jovial lunches in the company of like-minded chaps, which he had been led to expect, were things of the past, except, of course, for a charmed elite at the top of the ladder. The final curtain had come down long ago upon the last performance of a much-loved play. The actors had departed, the props had been dismantled and the theatre was now under new management.

Disenchanted, Rupert had left London for the provinces, but his current position with a firm of pension and insurance consultants in Cheltenham, while certainly more congenial, was really rather dull. He had substituted the motorway for a country lane with passing places – where nothing much of great interest passed.

Rupert yearned for something or someone to bring the sparkle back into his life – but what, who, where?

Distracted no doubt by this dismal train of thought, Rupert failed to notice that the car in front of him had slowed up and indicated an intention to turn into a private driveway coming up shortly on the left-hand side. On becoming belatedly aware of the danger, he braked and swerved but too late to avoid a collision. Both cars came to a halt.

I know all this as I was on the back seat of Lana's car. She'd taken me along to accompany her to an interview on local TV, no doubt to enhance the image that she wanted to project as a nice, cuddly person. I know all about Rupert's story, too, because later, when he became my master, I heard him talking about it with an old school chum.

Rupert clambered out of his car to review the damage, said that he was most dreadfully sorry and admitted that it was his fault.

Lana's chauffeur, a large, unpleasant, bearded man, rose from the driver's seat of the big top-of-the-range BMW, called poor Rupert a *stupid tosser* and was about to add further insults when Lana cut him short.

"Shurr up, Herbie," she said, beaming at Rupert. One look at him instantly would have told her that Rupert had class. It didn't need sartorial clichés like the old-fashioned tweed suit, the jaunty trilby and the old school tie to confirm this. It was somehow just obvious, and it was class, if you remember, with which Lana had a particular obsession.

For his part Rupert stood open-mouthed, dumbfounded, for he had recognised that the lady who had just emerged from the rear seat as none other than the gorgeous Lana Kendall, singer, dancer and star of at least five blockbuster movies, including the recent smash hit *Backstabber* – an adaptation for our times of *Macbeth* reworked as a steamy tale of sex, murder and boardroom intrigue with Lana herself, of course, in the role of the ambitious wife of the hapless new sales director. Sex symbol, pin-up – essential to the cash flow of every life-style magazine – Lana was the daily bread of a thousand *paparazzi*. In America she was acclaimed as the new Queen of Tinseltown.

Lana suggested that they both needed a drink after what had happened,and invited Rupert to follow her car.

Quite incapable of speech, Rupert nodded his acceptance.

The two, slightly battered vehicles drove in convoy down the long winding driveway through beautiful beech woods, coming eventually upon the great Victorian pile known as Loverham Hall.

Lana had purchased this slightly absurd edifice, half mock-medieval castle, half French château, from the trustees of a failing nursing home. Millions of pounds had since been expended upon its refurbishment. Acres of chintz, truckloads of gilded reproduction French empire-style furniture and herds of buffalo hide Chesterfield sofas were requisitioned; the grounds were enlivened with a riot of fountains, cascades and grottoes, and the building itself bristled with a forest of new spires, battlements and turrets. If Bombay had its Bollywood, thought Rupert, nearby Cheltenham now had its Chollywood.

Champagne cocktails led inevitably to an intimate candle-lit dinner. Dinner was followed inexorably by an offer of a bed for the night, *Lana's* bed, of course.

Descriptions of sex are generally as embarrassing as descriptions of fine wines are pretentious, and those of a prurient disposition would be far better off downloading *Napoleon meets Josephine* which gave Lana her first starring role. The graphic sex scenes bear a remarkable resemblance to occurrences at Loverham Hall later that evening and well into the night.

Making his departure from Lana the following morning with fond kisses and promises of an early reunion, Rupert was in an advanced state of euphoria. The vulgar extravagance of the revamped Loverham Hall somehow served as an antidote to the boring blandness which had in recent times afflicted his life. But much more to the point he was infatuated, indeed enraptured, with its owner. The collision the day before had been more than a mere traffic accident; two worlds had collided – the real world and the world of dreams. And Rupert knew which one he liked best.

As Lana watched him from the drawing-room window disappearing up the drive, she turned to Lawrence, her faithful secretary, by whose side I happened to be sitting, taking in every word.

"So, what do you make of my shining white knight, Larry?"
She asked.

"Major Torville seems to me a perfect gentleman, Madam,"
Lawrence replied, wincing slightly at being referred to as *Larry*, "and
according to my research, he is the scion of a most distinguished and
ancient family. Sir Hugo de Torville came over with the Conqueror."

"Yes, but there's distinguished and distinguished, Larry. You
have to, like, distinguish. You talk about this *Sir* Hugo ... they've
got a title then?"

"Well yes, Madam."

"... and what if I was to marry 'im – Rupert – I mean?"

"Marry him, Madam?"

"Calm down, Larry, just like supposing I was to, but, if it
happened, would I, like, one day become Lady Torville?"

"I'm afraid not, Madam, you see, it is Major Torville's uncle
who is the current baronet and it is his son, the Major's first cousin
Percy, who will inherit the title. It's Percy's wife who will become
Lady Torville."

"Well, that's not much frigging use, is it?"

"I'm very sorry, Madam. Will that be all?"

"Yeah ... but, wait! What about this man you called the
Conqueror who seems to be a friend of the family? Not mafia is
'e? Perhaps 'e's a Lord or something. Check 'im out will you, Larry.
We could always invite 'im to our Summer party, couldn't we?"

Rupert, however, had other ideas, as would soon become
painfully obvious.

Tirelessly, he had bombarded Loverham Hall with telephone
calls, emails and letters. Whoever answered the calls always
replied that Miss Kendall was *not at home*; and the letters and
emails went unanswered except for one short letter from
Lawrence politely explaining that Miss Kendall desired no further
contact with Rupert and enclosing a bill for the damage to the

BMW. Personal visits got no further than the main gate. An e-mail to Lana's agent in New York was met with threats of litigation but Rupert was, of course, much too much of a gentleman to threaten exposure of their brief relationship to the tabloid press.

Instead, believing that Lana's minions were trying to keep them apart, he embarked on a reckless mission to break into the Hall to see her. Using his military skills to evade the various security measures he nearly succeeded, but was apprehended by Herbert, the burly chauffeur, while endeavouring to climb through a ground floor window. Fisticuffs ensued and the Police were summoned. The headline next day in the *Gloucestershire Echo* read *Baronet's nephew stalks famous film star*.

About a week after this incident, Lawrence was taking me for a walk in the grounds on Lana's orders – not out of any concern for my welfare of course but because she was *effing fed up* of my barking. I always barked loudly when I wanted to go out and invariably Lana summoned poor Lawrence and told him to take *this stupid effing dog out of my sight*. As soon as we had passed through the formal gardens surrounding the house and had reached the field beyond, Lawrence let me off the lead to run around. It was then that I noticed a car parked in a lay-by just off the public road. There was high hedge along the road frontage which concealed Loverham Hall from view, but just at this point where the lay-by was located, the hedge thinned out and there was small gap.

I was certain that the car parked there belonged to Rupert. I'd seen him come down the drive with Lana after their collision in the road and I recalled that he had stayed that night. He had patted me on the head and said nice things about me and I had licked his hand. He seemed to me a very nice man. Sometime later there was that awful kerfuffle, when Rupert had come back and the horrible Herbert had punched him.

I could see that there was a man standing on the far side of the car and I felt sure that it was Rupert himself. Before Lawrence could stop me, I bounded away up towards the road and wormed my way through the little gap in the hedge.

I was right. The man was indeed Rupert – and he was leaning on the roof of the car holding a pair of binoculars. So engrossed was he in surveying the scene, no doubt in the hope of catching a glimpse of Lana, that he didn't notice me. By good fortune one of the car doors was open. I hopped in, unseen, and made myself comfortable on the rear seat.

Whether Rupert had planned another invasion of Loverham Hall or not I cannot say, but if he had he thought better of it. We drove away. He didn't notice me in the back of the car until he pulled into the car park of the block of flats in Cheltenham where he lived.

"What on earth are you doing here?" he asked.

I whimpered a little and cowered on the seat. I was terrified that he would drive me back to Loverham Hall.

But he didn't. I think it may have been the soulful look in my eyes at which dogs are so adept when they want to make a special appeal to their masters.

"Well, at least someone wants me," he said, "and if I can't have Lana I may as well keep you instead."

I have *never* been more relieved.

Rupert is a good master and I was blissfully happy to have found someone who cared for me and treated me as a proper dog. Poor Rupert, however, still moped and pined for Lana, and was distraught over his failure to see her again. Plainly, he had not been able to overcome his futile infatuation. My own happiness was offset by his obvious misery. I wished I could do something to help and, as it happened, an opportunity came my way.

It was a sunny Saturday morning and Rupert was taking me

for a walk as usual. It proved to be a *red-letter day,* a term, I understand, derived from old calendars in which feast days and other special days were highlighted in red. In my canine calendar, if I had such a thing, this Saturday would certainly be highlighted in red. (I think some would regard 'red-letter day' as a cliché but we dogs don't worry about that sort of thing.) In any event, we were walking through fashionable Montpelier in Cheltenham, when who should we come upon, sitting on a wall, but my old friend Jam. She too had managed to escape from Lana. She had ended up in a shelter for stray cats but, being a beautiful animal, had soon been re-homed with a retired stockbroker and his wife. Jam now lived in great comfort in the delightful Georgian terrace along which we just happened to be walking. She is no longer called Jam – any more than I am called Sponge. Her new name is Cleopatra and, given that cats are supposed to have originated in Egypt, an entirely appropriate one too for a true queen of cats.

My chance meeting with Jam – I mean Cleopatra – would have qualified the day as a red-letter day on its own account, but something else, even more important, was to happen just a few moments later which would make the day even a brighter shade of red.

As we turned the corner into the next street, I saw a lady coming towards us. She was not a dazzling beauty like Lana but, in my humble doggy view, she was in many ways more attractive. She had a lovely figure and the sweetest, roundest, freckly face you'll ever see. And with that special canine sense I possess, I could look beyond her outward appearance and see a person of a kind and gentle nature, quiet humour and homely disposition. It occurred to me immediately that she was the perfect cure for my master's obsession with Lana.

I was on one of those extendable types of lead and, before Rupert could control me, I had bounded forward and jumped up at the nice lady – leaving my muddy paw marks on her dress. And being caught by surprise and slightly off balance she all but fell over. I was sorry to have to do this, of course, but it was all in a good cause.

Rupert, with great presence of mind, rushed to her assistance and managed to catch her in his arms and prevent her from falling. I recall exactly the conversation which followed:

"I'm so sorry about my dog. I can't think what came over him … and, look, he's muddied your dress too. I shall of course pay for it to be cleaned."

"No, no … don't worry about that. It's an old dress anyway," she said.

"Oh, but I really must insist," Rupert replied. "My name's Rupert Torville by the way."

I could see a new light now in my master's eyes.

"And I'm Olivia Pendlebury."

"Well, Miss Pendlebury – it is *Miss* I suppose? I'm sorry, I don't mean to be rude … "

"Oh, yes, definitely Miss," Olivia replied emphatically.

I observed that Olivia's eyes, too, had taken on a sudden brightness and, with a shy smile, her face seemed even prettier than before.

"Well, Miss Pendlebury, er … Olivia. I must say you seem a bit shaken … not surprisingly. My beastly hound nearly bowled you over, the least I can do is to offer you a nice cup of coffee. There's a little place just a minute or two from here – the New Moon Café I think it's called – you probably know it …"

"Oh, that would be very kind, thank you."

And … another cliché coming up but – *wuff, wuff* – who cares? *The rest*, as they say, *is history.*

SIXTEEN

The Truth

Several weeks had passed and there had been no further incident involving the Colonel and Emily. I had kept a discreet eye on them during our evening sessions at the bar and once or twice I had thought they had exchanged what might be described as *meaningful glances*. But I had come to the conclusion that this was probably my imagination. The whole thing seemed to have fizzled out, if indeed there was ever anything to fizzle ... but I was wrong to be so complacent.

I had only just finished my supper one Friday evening when the telephone rang in the hall. It was my brother, Marcus. This was a bit odd. My brother usually only phoned, if he phoned at all, on Sundays. Must be something serious, I thought, and unfortunately, I was right.

"Look George, there's something I think you ought to know."

"Oh, yes?"

"I don't want to be telling tales out of school and it's really none of my business, but I feel I have to tell you this. I have an old pal of mine staying with me up here in London for the weekend and earlier this evening I went to Paddington to meet him off the train. And guess who I saw coming through the ticket barrier?"

"Well, how should I know?"

"It was your friend the Colonel, with your lovely barmaid Emily – if I've got her name right?"

"No! Really?"

"Yes, really. They walked across the concourse in the direction of the taxis, and I have to say that they seemed very lovey-dovey. He had his arm around her and she kissed him at least twice before they disappeared from view. I don't think they saw me."

"Oh, my God!"

"I do hope I've done the right thing in telling you, George. The Colonel seems such a nice old bloke to me, it would be quite awful if he got himself into the same ghastly mess as I did."

"Absolutely Marcus, quite right. Actually, there have been a few rumours about a relationship which, to be frank, I simply didn't believe until now. Clearly, something must be done … "

***

I knew that Emily would be away for the weekend. She had said she was going to London to visit her mother and the Colonel had said rather vaguely that he would be tied up over the weekend and not be at the Back Bar again until Monday. Well, it seemed that they both had a rather particular plan in mind.

I lost no time in phoning Tom and Desmond to arrange a council of war for the following morning at the Harbour Café, where it was unlikely that we would be overheard.

"Sorry, chaps, it looks as if you were right all along and I was wrong," I said.

"Jesus!" Said Desmond.

"What are we going to do about it?" Tom asked.

"Well, we'll have to say something now to persuade him that this is not a good thing at all. One or both of them will end up getting hurt. This is a small town. Can you imagine what people will say if it all comes out? We can't allow the Colonel to make a fool of himself. It won't be at all easy, but we've got to give it a try at least."

"Who's going to do the talking, then?" Tom said.

"Well, don't look at me!" Said Desmond emphatically, "I shall be totally pissed!"

"Well, that's nothing new!" Tom said. "But, come to think of it, in the circumstances not a bad idea. Seriously though, this is a job for you, George. You're the lawyer, the man of words. You'll know how to put things properly. And we'll back you up ... "

"Well, thanks a million," I said. I knew instinctively, of course, that it would end up with me.

"But, how," Tom continued, "are we going to set up a meeting? Can't very well do it at the pub."

"I've given some thought to that," I said. "When we all meet in the bar on Monday evening as usual, we'll say that the three of us are going for a curry afterwards at the Star of India and invite the Colonel to join us. I'm sure he'll agree to come. It's not the night he plays bridge and it's unlikely he'd have any other engagement on a Monday."

"Good idea!"

***

Thus, the three of us, Tom, Desmond and myself, were sitting by the bar on Monday evening, nervously awaiting the arrival of the Colonel. We were there slightly earlier than usual by prior arrangement. Emily seemed to be her normal charming self and must have wondered why we were all so much quieter than normal.

The Colonel was always punctual and on the dot of six o'clock he duly arrived. He bore a wide grin on his ruddy face.

"Hello there, Chaps," he said in his jovial, booming voice. "I have an important announcement to make."

Oh, my God, I thought, we're too late.

He motioned to Emily who came out from behind the bar to stand close beside him.

"I would like to introduce you," he said, putting a loving arm around her, "to my darling *daughter*."

"Good God!" Said Tom.

"Awww!" I said.

"Holy Mary, Mother of God!" said Desmond.

"I suppose I'd better explain," the Colonel said. "But first I should apologise to you for keeping all this quiet until now – I didn't want to say anything until I was quite sure of the facts and all the loose ends were tied up ... "

LET ME BEGIN WITH THE VERY FIRST DAY that Emily served in the bar. As soon as I saw her, I was struck by her resemblance to a lady I once knew, at the time the love of my life.

Many years ago, I was home on leave from Germany and I met a young lady at a party – Harriet Weekes was her name. I fell for her instantly and the very next evening I asked her out to dinner. One thing led to another and we ended up at her flat and, well, I spent the night there. In fact, I spent the rest of my leave there. Although we had only just met, I had fallen hopelessly in love with her – a love which I believed was entirely reciprocated. It was a wrench when I had to return to my unit in Germany but I promised to write and I did many times – but there was no response. I was both frustrated and saddened as you might imagine.

As soon as my next leave came round, I rushed straight round to Harriet's flat, and it was only then that I realised my mistake ... I had addressed all my letters to Bentham Road; the correct address was Bentham *Gardens*. There is a Bentham Road in the vicinity where my letters had, no doubt, ended up, but they never found their way to Bentham Gardens nor were they returned. Unfortunately, by this time Harriet had moved on without leaving any forwarding address. Despite numerous enquiries I simply couldn't trace her. I had, of course, no idea that she had become pregnant.

Harriet had been in a long-term relationship with a man called Robert Turner but they had parted company shortly before I first met her at the party. When she didn't hear from me, she assumed that I had lost interest in her and after a little while resumed her relationship with Robert. In fact, she left her flat and moved in with him and later they were married. Emily was born and Robert accepted her as his child. Emily would always have understood that Robert was her father – she had really no reason to think otherwise. Harriet, however, strongly suspected that it was I who was the father, *and* she believed that Robert nurtured the same suspicion although they never talked about it. Sadly, the marriage didn't last and Harriet and Robert were divorced.

Frankly, when I first saw Emily I didn't know what to do. She was the spitting image of the young woman I had met all those years ago, but was this just a coincidence? In the end, I plucked up the courage to speak to her. She came round to see me at home, bringing with her a recent photograph of her mother which we compared with one that Harriet had given me during our brief relationship. Despite the passage of time, one could see that it was quite obviously the same person – and Emily confirmed that her mother's maiden name was Weekes. Emily gave me Harriet's address and I wrote to her explaining the awful mix-up over the street name and saying how very sorry I was.

As a bluff old soldier I'm not given to having emotional conversations – except for heated rows with tradesmen who fail to turn up when they promise – but when a few days after posting my letter to Harriet, I received a call from her, this was certainly one such occasion and I shall never forget it. She told me briefly all that had happened in her life since we last met and how she would love to see me again. Then she dropped the bombshell – she was quite sure, she said, that Emily was my daughter. To say that I was bowled over would be the understatement of the century.

At first Harriet was reluctant for anything to be said that might upset Emily, but finally she agreed. And Emily took the news very well – in fact she seemed happy to have found her real father. After all, she could barely remember Robert and had not seen or heard from him since the divorce. DNA tests proved my paternity.

This last weekend, I travelled with Emily to London and finally met Harriet again – mother, father and daughter all together for the first time. It was indeed a very moving moment."

"And," the Colonel continued after wiping his brow, "I have a further important announcement to make: Harriet is coming to live with me here in Bufferton – and we are to be married in the Spring."

There were others in the bar that evening besides the four of us regulars – and yet all chatter ceased as the Colonel spoke. There was a brief pause, as everyone took in all they had heard, followed by a great chorus of cheers and much thunderous clapping. There was not a dry eye in the place.

I cast a sideways glance at Tom and Desmond who, I sensed, were clearly looking to me to say something. Somehow, I managed to compose myself.

"We have heard many stories in this bar," I said. "Some with happy endings but some which end in disaster. The story we've heard today, however, has the happiest of all endings. I'm sure everyone here tonight will want to join me in offering both the Colonel, Emily and Harriet our sincerest good wishes and many congratulations!"

There was a further chorus of "Hear, hear" and more clapping all round.

"Champagne urgently needed," called Desmond, "lots of it!" And who were we to disagree?

SEVENTEEN

Life Goes On

Autumn has arrived. The summer visitors have gone and the town once again belongs to its residents. We still get the occasional stranger in the back bar with a tale to tell, but not so often, and this evening there are only locals. Tom, Desmond, the Colonel and I sit with a drink in hand.

Emily has started her job in Plymouth as a primary school teacher and we have a new barmaid. Her name is Gemma. She is not as sexy as Gloria or as beautiful as Emily but she's cheerful, good-humoured and pretty and we count ourselves very fortunate. It so happens that she used to help with the breakfasts at Gull View where Harry, the famous travel writer, spent so much time writing about his imaginary adventures in distant lands, about larger-than-life people he never met and who never existed and about exotic places he never visited. A nice twist: Charles, who revealed Harry's secret to us, has become engaged to Alice, Harry's niece. Charles now lives at Gull View and has become one of our regulars at the Sloop.

RUMOURS FINALLY SURFACED in political and media circles, possibly as a result of a leak from someone at the Home Office, that a so-called mind-reading device known as the Cyclops Machine was under consideration by the Government for use by the security services. There had been questions in the House: *Would this not be the greatest intrusion ever upon privacy and individual freedom?*

The Home Secretary, called to the despatch box, did his best to assuage Members' concerns. He maintained that the potential benefits of this device would far outweigh the theoretical problems. He insisted *Only those with something to hide have anything to fear.*

Tom was not impressed: "That's always the cry of meddling minsters, bossy bureaucrats and prying policeman the world over." I entirely agreed, mindful of the man with the funny watch and his warning about policemen wearing baseball caps.

PAUL, WHO TOLD US ABOUT THE INVISIBILITY of his former friend Max, visited the pub again just a few days after he had told us his story but this time in the company of his wife. When he entered the bar, poor Paul was very red in the face, breathing heavily and his shirt dripping with sweat. We guessed that his wife had insisted on accompanying him on his walk and no back-sliding had been permitted – probably, we thought, he had been forced to walk the whole way along the cliffs to Bufferton Cove and back again without a break for refreshment. Limping slightly he came up to the bar and, with a despairing glance in our direction, ordered two glasses of fizzy water.

A month or so later, to our surprise, Paul turned up once more in our bar. He had come for a further short stay at The Bufferton Sands Hotel, which he clearly rated highly. On this occasion, however, he was on his own. His wife had gone off to Barcelona with her sister for a long weekend. This time, he said, he would be able truly to enjoy his stay, without fear of being forced to torture himself in the hotel gym or take long and arduous walks along the cliffs.

I asked if he'd ever seen Max again. No, he hadn't, he said. Max had disappeared once more, though whether he was still hiding in plain sight as before, he was unsure. There had been a rumour that Max had been spotted in a bar by the harbour in Portofino on the Italian Riviera. Perhaps the cloak of invisibility had finally worn a bit thin and he'd had to do a bunk overseas after all.

MARTIN, THE UNFORTUNATE MAN who had left his diary behind, never came back for it. It is still behind the bar.

TOM, ON A TRIP TO SCOTLAND to visit relatives, happened to tune into the local TV news one evening. There was a report that the police were searching for a man calling himself Roger MacDuff, wanted for questioning about an alleged fraud involving the renting of a castle to an American family. MacDuff had apparently referred the family to a website with an image of a fairytale Scottish castle by a beautiful loch, surrounded by heather-clad hills and described as a 'luxury Highland retreat'. They had paid MacDuff a substantial deposit in advance but when they arrived in Scotland from New York discovered that the 'castle' was, as the reporter rather wittily put it, *a castle in the air*. It simply didn't exist. Attempts to contact MacDuff met with no success and he was nowhere to be found. It was reported that MacDuff – who claimed to be a Scottish Laird – was last seen at a hotel in Edinburgh. He had left in the early hours of the morning without paying his bill – just two days before the arrival of the Americans.

We all strongly suspected that Roger MacDuff was none other than that old cheat and charmer Roger Duffy, in another guise.

NELSON, THE PUB CAT, received a postcard with a picture of Big Ben signed *Emma* – the very special cat who played the starring role in one of the stories we were told.

It is dark outside now, but the sky is clear and starry and there is a full moon. The town's charming little harbour is all illuminated and looks all the prettier for it. In the distance one can just discern the dark outline of the headland thrusting itself like a giant fist, far out into the moonlit shimmering sea. All is well with the world.

"Tell you what," said Desmond, "I've had a brilliant idea."

"Oh, my God!" said Tom.

"No really I have," Desmond went on. "You know all the stories we've heard in this bar? Well, we could write them down in a proper fashion and publish them in a book to be called, say, *Tales told at the Sloop Inn* or something. It would be bound to sell millions of copies and probably get translated into at least fifteen languages. The royalties would be colossal, shared equally between us, of course. We'd be drinking champagne every night for the rest of our lives!"

"Absolutely not," I said, "that's a quite outrageous suggestion. These stories were told to us in confidence in the privacy of our little bar. Publishing them would be quite unthinkable. I wouldn't dream of it, not in a thousand years."

"I couldn't agree with you more, George," said Tom.

"Hmm, well I suppose you're right. Pity though all the same," said Desmond in a tone of resignation. "Gracious me!" he said, abruptly changing the subject "Look at the time. Best be off home now."

"Me, too," said the Colonel following Desmond to the door. "I'm taking Harriet out to dinner this evening at the Bufferton Sands."

Only Tom and I remained.

"Time for another?" Asked Tom.

"Well, I suppose so, since you ask," I said. "Just a quick one!"

www.ingramcontent.com/pod-product-compliance
Lightning Source LLC
Chambersburg PA
CBHW040537170726
48295CB00012B/496